MW01248853

Eight Moments

Carmen L. Hendrix

Magnolia Babies Publishing
Miami, Florida

EIGHT MOMENTS

Copyright© 2017 by Magnolia Babies Publishing

MAGNOLIA BABIES

PUBLISHING

ISBN: 978-0-9978060-2-1
Library of Congress Catalog Number: 2017911457

Published in the United States by Magnolia Babies Publishing LLC, Florida
www.MagnoliababiesPublishing.com

DEDICATED to my family and friends who have supported me along the way and all of my readers who have remained true, and waited patiently, for this novel. You are truly an inspiration!

FOREWORD

Carmen Hendrix has penned a masterpiece. This book is filled with all the expectations that a reader seeks when choosing their next good read. It is overflowing with deep sentiments that prick the heart at the seat of all emotions. It touches on the main elements of real family life with its disappointments, unfulfilled expectations, forgiveness and the lack of, emotional abuse, infidelity, and even unconditional love. Her insight to put such on-point dialogue to an absolutely captivating storyline is simply amazing. Her approach to describing feelings and passions that connect the pain of loss and the yearnings of dreams that don't die is remarkable. *Eight Moments* leaves the reader hungry for more, it is "gooder" than good; it is GREAT!!!

Jaki Rivon, Poet

-1-

Red Sneakers and Blue Trim

The grocery store is my favorite place. Doritos. Check. Hot sauce. Check. Wait...Louisiana Hot sauce. Check. I normally like to shop the perimeters of the grocery store but today I need a treat. It's been a long day. Actually, it's been a hard day. The conversation I had with my boss this morning still lingers in my thoughts like it just happened.

"Ms. Catchings, you replied to Tom's email and said that you don't have anything to add to the report. You didn't add anything to the report in the first place," she said to me.

"Actually, I am the one who created the report. Tom was supposed to add his information and send it to you. I sent you the first version last week."

"I don't have it."

EIGHT MOMENTS

"It's there."

"I. Don't. Have. It. And you need to be doing your job instead of going around telling people that I don't like you. Ms. Catch-ings." There it was, the reason for her call in the first place. She was looking for a reason to vent about something she'd heard. Petty. I would've asked if she was out of her mind, but I decided to settle on the fact that the lady is just a mess and some of her antics have to be ignored if I am going to keep my job. However, if she'd said my name like that one more time, I was going to scream because just hearing the sound of her voice irritated me this morning so, purposely mispronouncing my name, wasn't helping the situation. Aside from that, I haven't taken the time to talk to anyone at work to say anything about whether she does or doesn't like me and, though I know she is a trip-and-a-half, I was really trying to wrap my head around the fact that she seriously called me with he-said/she-said stuff!

"Hello. Ms. Catchings. Can you hear me?" she asked, interrupting my thought.

CHAPTER 1

"Yes. I can hear you and I didn't say that Melanie."

"Well, I heard the same thing from four people on the team and they are four people I trust," she said with an attitude.

"Perhaps you need to re-evaluate who you trust," I said snidely, returning the favor.

"Excuse me Ms. Catch-ings?" She sounded puzzled, like she couldn't believe I'd just said that to her so I followed up with, "I didn't say that to anyone because I haven't had the chance to talk to anyone on the team Melanie. Let's move on. Were you able to find the email I sent last week? I can forward it to you again if you'd like."

"Yes. I have it. Thank you." She hung up the phone and I shook my head. I knew she was fuming because she didn't even apologize for the accusations. But then again, I didn't expect one. That's who she is. After all, this *is* the woman who had the audacity ask me about some petty gossip she'd heard and had just talked to me as if she questioned *my* character. I don't know what her beef is with me but I can say that she is, without a shadow of a doubt, a textbook case of a person who abuses her authority and I have to get a new job. The menacing tone in her voice during that conversation served as a reminder that I need to hurry up and start looking.

Since the first day she talked to me, Melanie has treated me like she hates me. She comes after me constantly, even trying to embarrass me on conference calls. It's like she is unleashing her wrath on me and, to be honest, it is unwarranted. Everything she does is intentional and deliberate, like she is trying to make an example out of the new kid on her block. I say *her* block, because I have been doing this job for years, just not under her leadership. I was just moved to her team a few months ago. This is a person with whom I have never even had a face-to-face meeting, even after several attempts. So, I don't understand her beef and just thinking about the conversation infuriates me. I try to hold back my anger but it is starting to settle in my bones and my blood feels like it is rushing to my head. I become hot and

CHAPTER 1

anxious just thinking about it. I wish I had told her how I really felt and hit her with a little gossip I'd heard too, probably from those same team members she *trusts*; that she'd been married and divorced twice, with her second marriage lasting less than a year. Based on that alone, she has a poor track record when it comes to judging someone's character traits. It's funny how you don't have to talk to people to hear the gossip they spread. But, I chose to err on the side of caution, and kept my mouth closed, since she has my job in her hands. At age thirty, I know when to rock the boat and when to stay put.

Deciding to put her, and that conversation, out of my mind, I continue my shopping. Eggs. Milk. Chicken. Lamb. Brown Rice. Mushrooms. Spinach. Lemons. Ginger Root. Cherry Tomatoes. Strawberries. Blueberries. I now have everything on my list. I walk towards the front registers and wait in the checkout line, when a man approaches from behind. He towers me, and I can see his massive shadow on the floor in front of me. I quickly look back to glance at this person who is making me look so tiny because, at a little over six feet, I am taller than most women. He is on the phone telling his girlfriend, I assume, about how much he misses and loves her just moments before he disconnects the call and taps me on my shoulder.

"Hey miss lady," he says.

I turn and look up at him before saying, "Hello. How are you?"

He looks at me and smiles and I can't contain the thought that he is just another trifling man.

"I'm well," I say without returning the favor of asking how he is doing, my normal routine in an exchange of niceties. Flirting with me so blatantly after talking to someone on the phone in front of me is just, well its infuriating, no matter how polite he is. I reach up to brush my curls back and sigh, hoping it will show my disinterest, but he doesn't notice as he shuffles through his pocket when his phone begins to ring again. He answers, "Hey baby…baby…baby did you mean to call me right back?" He pauses for a moment and then disconnects only to dial

CHAPTER 1

the number again. The person ahead of me moves closer to the cashier and everyone in line shifts forward. He places his phone on speaker while he gathers the items he'd placed on the floor which indicates that he clearly meant to run in to grab a few items but ended up with more than expected. His phone blares out a loud ring and then a small girl answers the line.

"Hello," she says.

I turn towards him and I am instantly blinded by the radiant smile that appears when he hears the young girl's voice. His tall frame exudes happiness as he responds, "Hey baby. Did you mean to call daddy back, or was it an accident by your mom?"

"Hey daddy. Mommy may have done it."

"Ok. May I speak to your mommy?"

"Yes sir. Hold on please."

His daughter sounds like she is adorable and if she looks anything like him, she probably is. I can't help but acknowledge that the man is attractive.

EIGHT MOMENTS

His massive frame is muscle-toned and solid and he looks so good in his suit that he's caught the eye of quite a few women in the store. The cashier even did a double-take once she notices him in her line, patting her hair down to make herself look more presentable. That was smart, because a part of it was sticking up and you could see her weave track in the top of her head. She looks stressed, like she needs a break. I look back to try to help him gather his items and put them in my basket but I am still bothered by the fact that he tried to make conversation with me after talking to his woman and their child. He mouths the words "thank you" to me and scoots the package of water he has towards me so that he can walk forward without leaving it behind.

I cannot, for the life of me, understand why the grocery store has twenty-five lines and only three open. That's why the cashier is stressed. As a manager, you see your customers waiting, why not make it convenient for them and open more lines? To make matters worse, two of the three open lanes are for ten

CHAPTER 1

items or less. The sound of the ringing of the groceries becomes a little louder. Bloop. Bloop. Bloop. I turn back towards the cashier as the lady on the phone blurts out, "Hello." She sounds like she does not want to talk to him. He stutters, "Ummmm…what time can I pick her up this afternoon?" She responds, "I will be at my house around five. You can get her at six." Her voice is flat, emotionless and anyone can tell she has zero interest in continuing this conversation. I guess I can nix the idea that he was talking to his woman and their child. Now I feel bad. Before he can say anything else to her, she has already passed the phone back to the little girl and you can hear her in the background saying, "Your daddy will get you at six o'clock. Ok?" The little girl begins to talk to him again until her mommy tells her to get her ice cream treat in the kitchen and she tells him she has to go. He smiles but seems troubled as he says goodbye. I'd be troubled if I were him, she'd just said she wasn't home, maybe she was at a friend's house. We move closer to the cashier and he apologizes for the interruption and thanks me again for helping him with his items.

"No problem," I say to him.

"Do you come to this store often?" He asks.

"Yes."

"I have never seen you here before. It is nice to have run into you today."

"You too." I say, feeling bad for labeling him as a trifling brother.

We stand there for a few moments in silence with the bloop of the registers and the elevator music from the grocery store keeping us occupied, and you can tell he is contemplating what he should say to me next. He takes a breath to start a sentence a few times but he never does and, since my back is turned, I don't turn around to see what he is doing. I move closer to the cashier yet again. I hear him take a few deep breaths again, before he asks, "Do you mind if I call you sometime?" I turn around and look at him to confirm that he is speaking to me and he smiles before saying, "I know it is kind of forward but...do you mind?" I stand

CHAPTER 1

there for a moment, thinking about his interaction with his daughter. He seems to have a good relationship with her so I guess it is worth trying. Besides, I have been so busy organizing community events with JoAnn, and working for a woman who is narcissistic and certifiably crazy, that I have neglected any chance of being in a relationship or even getting to know a man. I smile at him and then I think about how dry his child's mother was on the phone when she spoke to him and I decide I don't want any drama. I pause before speaking and he interrupts by saying, "I just want a few moments of your time." I smile again and ask him for his phone so that I can type my number in it before saying, "My name is Donna." He smiles, "Hi Donna. I'm Stephen. Thank you." I'm impressed by his politeness and we continue to make small talk until I reach the register. He offers to pay for my groceries in exchange for helping him in the line but I decline and tell him I will speak with him soon before I walk away. I can't wait to get home. I have a bag of Doritos and hot sauce calling my name and

I can't wait to eat them. Maybe this day isn't so bad after all. I pick up the phone to dial my good friend JoAnn before I drive off so that I can tell her about the gentleman I'd just met. But, after a few rings, her voicemail picks up. Dang it. I then call Sierra, my sister. "Hey Donna," she answers excitedly. I smile. It is always good to talk to my sisters and my dad. "What are you doing?" I ask as I put my car in reverse. I watch in the rearview mirror as Stephen pushes his cart in the parking lot. He looks like he is looking for something. Sierra interrupts my moment of curiosity by saying, "Nothing much. I just got off work and Chandler and I are about to go see mom. She is about to be discharged from the hospital. Daddy is there with her now."

"The hospital? What happened?" I ask.

"We thought she was having a stroke, but she wasn't. As of now, they can't seem to find anything wrong with her."

"Really?"

CHAPTER 1

"Yes. Are you going to come home to see about her?" She has got to be kidding. She knows there is no way in the world I will ever willingly go home to see about my mother. Not the one who mistreated me for years. No way.

"Ummm…my phone is ringing Sierra. Let me call you back."

"Really Donna? Don't act like that. This is our mom."

"I'll think about it. I will call you back."

"Ok."

"Give me ten minutes."

"Ok." She sounds defeated as she hangs up. The phone rings again and I answer, "Hello."

"Hey Ms. Lady." He sounds even better on the phone than I thought he would. "Hi Stephen. This is a pleasant surprise," I say.

"Yes. I was hoping to run into you in the parking lot. I am on my way to pick up my daughter. She lives about 30 minutes away so I will be there early because if I am one minute late, her mother goes berserk."

EIGHT MOMENTS

"How old is your daughter?"

"She is five."

"Wow. A little diva, hunh?"

"You have no idea." He laughs a little.

"Well you have plenty of time to get there."

"Yes. Yes, I do. But I'd rather be early, than late. I don't like drama and her mother is full of it. I try to do everything by the book to keep everyone happy."

Check mark for him. He doesn't like drama and tries to avoid it at all cost. This is his second one in a matter of minutes. I thought it was quite noble of him to offer to pay for my groceries. That did not go unnoticed. We continue our small talk for about fifteen minutes or so until he receives a call. "Donna, may I call you back later this evening. I need to take this call?" he asks. "Sure," I say. We hang up after our goodbyes. I'm actually glad because I am just getting home and as much as I'd like to continue to get to know him, I'd rather have a moment of peace. I push the button to let the garage door up and then I slowly drive in, watching as the

CHAPTER 1

garage door goes down. I want to call my sister back and she is going to be upset that I haven't. But, I really don't know what to say to her. How do you ask about someone who has given zero thought about you and your well-being? How can you show a mother love when you know she will show nothing in return? The thought of this drives me crazy as I grab my grocery bags out of the car. I unlock the door and walk into the kitchen, placing the bags on the counter when the phone rings again. This time it's daddy. Damn. I know Sierra put him up to this. She knows that I am a sucker for daddy and if he asks, I will try to make it happen. The only thing he has never been able to do, is get me to come back to visit that house. No sir, it isn't happening.

"Hello," I answer.

"Hey Bay-girl." He sounds different, like he may be worried.

"Hey daddy."

"Listen. You need to come home. Chandler and Sierra are already looking for flights for you."

"Come home? Why?"

EIGHT MOMENTS

"It's your mother. We are going to have to move her to a hospice care facility. She doesn't have long to live and she wants to…uh. She asked to see you."

"She *asked* to see me?" I turn the phone towards me to make sure that I am really talking to my father. My mother hasn't shown interest in me since my brother Sam died and now, suddenly, she wants to see me? I say, "I love you daddy, but I don't want to see her. She will be fine and there is no need for a kumbaya moment. It is hard for…" I stop talking. "It is hard for what?" he asks. I want to say to him that it is hard for evil to die but refrain from disrespecting his love choices. After all, if he never fell in love with her, there would be no me. At least I know where my mean streak comes from. "It's hard for me to come home daddy." There is a long, awkward silence until he says, "Donna. You have to let it go. If you don't it will eat you alive. That is what happened to your mother. Do you want it to happen to you?" I begin to think of every way I could get out of going home but none seem good enough to tell my

CHAPTER 1

father so I finally concede. Well, there goes my "he will never get me to come home" stance. "I talked to Sierra earlier today and she said mom was on her way home. What changed?"

"That's just what I told Sierra and Chandler so they wouldn't worry before they got here. You really need to come home. I won't say more over the phone." He has a way of making me feel bad when I don't want to do what he has asked. I feel defeated now so I suck it up and say, "It'll be good to see you daddy. I will get packed and catch the next flight out." He seems pleased that he doesn't have to fight me on this and says, "Good then. One of your sisters will call you to see which flight works for you."

"Daddy I can get my flight."

"I'm sure you can. But you always pay for us to come see you so let me return the favor. It's important."

Knowing not to continue to argue with daddy once his mind is made up is something I learned years ago so I oblige him and we hang up the phone. I need a drink. I send a text to JoAnn to tell her I need to talk to her and then send one to my other good friend Maggie to tell her that I am home but need to postpone our Thursday "binge night." If no one else understands me, they do. JoAnn and I have been very close since the death of her son. We are both very active in the community, spreading awareness about citizens' rights. Since she'd just lost her son, and my mother and I aren't close, we bonded almost instantly and I don't know what I would do without her. She keeps me leveled and centered and has always encouraged me to try to make amends with my mom. She always says that she understands how I feel but she also knows how it feels to lose a son and asks me to be more sympathetic towards her. I was there to witness her grief when she lost her son, but I was there when she worked through it and her grieving process was completely different from my mom's. I never took the time to tell her everything that my mom did to me as I was growing up because it's something I'd rather forget.

I go to my bedroom to pack some clothes and shower. I look at my phone

CHAPTER 1

and see three missed calls. One is from my sister Chandler, one is a number I don't recognize, and the other is from my boss. What in the hell does *she* want? I pick up the phone to listen to my messages.

Message one: "Donna this is Chandler. Call me back so we can book your flight. I found one for late tonight or we can schedule tomorrow morning." I save the message.

Message two: "Ms. Catchings, you have won a grand prize trip for two to the Bahamas. Press one for more details." I delete the message. I didn't enter a contest to win a trip to the Bahamas and I am not getting sucked into a scheme now.

Message three: "Ms. Catch-ings. This is Melanie Baker. I know it is after-hours but I want to talk to you about this report. I need to get some information from you so that I can update my records for my meeting tomorrow with my boss." I save the message. I don't ever delete her messages, until I can write them down, word for word, and document the time. I don't trust her. I guess I will call her back first so I can tell her that I am going to Georgia.

I dial Melanie's number and she answers after the first ring. I think to myself, since you trust Tom so damn much, why in the hell can't you ask him? Oh, I know, because he didn't do the report and can't tell you his butt from a hole in the wall. The dislike I have for her is so intense that a trip to Georgia doesn't seem so bad. The way she says my name scrapes the inside of my veins, causing me to feel like I am bleeding from the inside out. It's truly cringe worthy. I can't wait to be rid of her for a few days.

"Ms. Catch-ings I see you got my message."

"I did. How can I help you?"

"Is everything alright?"

"I am fine. I was calling you back."

"Yes. I need you to explain your report to me so that I can be prepared for my meeting with my boss tomorrow." I provide an explanation to her about the orders my clients have placed and take a moment to forward her the charts I used

CHAPTER 1

to gather the data on their current managed services. I go into detail about the time frame on the projects we are working on and give her the information for the project manager. I even pass along a few templates I created because they make my job so much easier. "You are very detailed Ms. Catchings." Surprisingly, she says my name correctly. "Thank you," I say to her and continue, "Actually, I am glad you called. I just found out that my mother is not well and is being moved for hospital care. I will need to take a few vacation days to fly out to see her. I'm leaving tonight. I will have my laptop with me in case I am needed but I hope to use that time to focus on my family." Without hesitation, she tells me to take all of the time I need and follows it with, "Family is important Donna and I am sorry to hear about your mother." I thank her and hang up the phone.

I place call number two to Chandler.

"Hey sis. How are you?" she asks upon answering the phone.

"I'm good. I miss you," I say to her.

"I miss you too. Sierra is here with me and we are trying to book your flight through Southwest Airlines. What day is good for you?"

"Am I on speaker phone?"

"Yep."

"You can book the late flight for tonight. I'm already packed and can head to the airport right away. What time does it leave?"

"It leaves at 10:45 pm. I know I'm talking to you now, but we can catch up when you get here."

"Ok. That gives me 2 ½ hours. I can head out now. I have airline mileage points. I can use them so daddy won't have to pay for the ticket. Let me log on."

"Ok."

I find the ticket and pay for it with my airline points and ask Chandler to pick me up from the airport. Sierra starts talking to me in the background about not calling her back before I can apologize. "I'm sorry sis. I got sidetracked and had to call my boss back," I say. She forgives me

CHAPTER 1

after telling me that we will catch up when I make it home and we hang up. Finally, I have a moment to myself. I grab my bag and slip on my shoes. My Doritos and hot sauce are going to have to wait for me to come home. I was really looking forward to eating them. Disappointed, I do a once over to make sure I have put way all of the groceries and have everything I need.

This thing about my mom is starting to bother me and right on cue, before I can ask, Sierra sends me a text message to confirm that my mother really does want to talk to me and that she keeps asking for me.

I pick up the phone and dial Stephen. He answers after the first ring, "I was just about to call you," he says.

"Were you?" I don't wait for an answer before I continue, "I called to tell you that I need to postpone that lunch date we discussed earlier. I have an emergency and need to go home to check on my family. I don't know when I will be back."

"I'm sorry to hear that Donna. I hope all is well. Call me when you get a chance. When are you leaving?"

"I'm actually on my way to the airport now. My father says I need to get there as soon as possible."

"Have a safe flight. Call or text me when you land, it doesn't matter how late it is. Ok?"

"Sure," I say. His concern is pleasantly surprising. But I can't help but wonder if it is all a façade. My thought is interrupted by the sound of his daughter's voice as she asks, "Who is that daddy?" I laugh. "I will call you tomorrow Stephen. Enjoy your time with your daughter."

"No. Please. Let me know you made it safely tonight."

"I will. I don't know when I will be back home."

"We will figure something out. I have to go to Atlanta in a few weeks for work. So hopefully you will back before then because I may be out there for a couple of weeks."

CHAPTER 1

"Well I will be right outside of Atlanta. If I am still there, you may catch me."

He laughs and says he hopes so and after a moment's pause, I tell him I will call him and hang up the phone. My mind is still baffled by the thoughts of my mother and, to be honest, the thought of her asking to see me *specifically* is bothering me. The last time my mom said she wanted to see me, she really hurt me.

I remember the day vividly. It was the day after my brother died. Carrying around the memory of feeling the weight of Sam's body on mine as he protected me from the gunman still weighs heavily on me and it seems like my mother never understood, or cared, that I was traumatized by it. The guy that killed my brother had on some shoes that I will never forget, red sneakers with blue trim and the number 23 on them. They were shoes you didn't see often in my neighborhood. Imagine my surprise when my mother called me outside to see the face, and the shoes, that killed my brother. He was standing there, chatting with her and laughing as if he'd never done anything wrong and hadn't just killed someone the night before. How could she not know it was him? I told her about the shoes the night Sam died. I told her the red shoes killed Sam. Why would she stand there and talk to him? I stood frozen in the doorway for minutes before she even noticed I was there. She motioned for me to come outside, telling me that she wanted me to meet someone. My legs felt heavy with every step I took towards him, like I was walking in thick, muddy waters. Red Shoes stopped smiling when he saw me. It was like he'd seen a ghost.

"This is your daughter?" He asked my mom in a calm voice.

"Yes. It is." She eyed him closely before she motioned for me to come over.

"That was your son that got killed at the store yesterday?"

"Yes, it was." Her face saddened as she spoke to him and looked down at his shoes. She looked at me and said, "This is your cousin, Donna. Give him a hug."

CHAPTER 1

"Cousin?" I was puzzled. "This is our cousin," I asked.

"Yes Donna."

"But this is the…"

"Donna," she cut me off before I could finish the sentence, "This is my cousin. I wanted you to meet him. He just moved here a few weeks ago. Run along now." She pushed me towards the door and watched me as I gazed back at Sam's killer. She never said his name. Once I made it inside, she turned to him and told him she was sad about losing Sam and told him her heart was broken. After a brief pause, I heard her say, "If I'd lost that one, I wouldn't feel as bad." She looked back towards the door I'd just entered, not knowing I was still there, listening through the screen. She snickered slightly and my heart sunk as tears fell from my eyes. How can a mother not care if she lost a child? I will never forget it. A few days later, at the funeral, Red Shoes was there to offer his condolences but my mother would not speak to him, nor would she allow him inside. My father seemed to know who he was and was baffled about why my mom didn't want him there. "Isn't that Ingrid's boy?" he asked her. She shook her head as tears fell and told him to make sure he was gone and to never let him in the house. She reached over and hugged me as she whispered in my ear, "I should have let him kill you but I don't want your father to have to bear the burden of losing two children." I yanked away from her and slid closer to my daddy, knowing, at that very moment, that my mom tried to set me up when she called me to come outside.

I later found out that she'd anonymously turned my cousin in to the police for killing Sam. I couldn't sleep one night and got up to go to the kitchen for some water when I heard her talking to my father. She told him that there were few people she hated in this world and her cousin was one of them. "She was terrified when she saw him Gabe," she said to my father. "I knew he had done it and the look on her face was confirmation. He killed our boy Gabe. He killed him with no remorse and I want him to rot for it." The floor creaked as I moved towards them and she shot me an evil look, the

CHAPTER 1

same one she gave me when she previously told me that she wished I was dead.

As I arrive at the airport, I snap back to reality and call Maggie to fill her in on what has transpired. She knows everything that has happened with my mother throughout my life so she knows that this trip is hard for me. No longer wanting to talk about why I am going to Georgia, I divert the conversation and ask, "Can you use your key to pick up my car because I have no idea how long I will be gone? I can just get an Uber ride when I get back." After confirming that Maggie will pick up my car, I tell her how much I appreciate her and that I will call her once I get settled.

I grab my bag out of the trunk and head towards Southwest Airlines and I realize that I am starting to obsess over this thing with my mom. How can every part of me dislike her so much when every part of me has always wanted her to show me she loves me like she loves everyone else?

-2-

The Mall

The airport is a hustle. They make you pay to park, you have to give the guy a tip to handle your bags, then you pay extra to go through the TSA line a little quicker so you won't miss the flight that has already cost you a gazillion dollars, especially a last minute one. And don't find yourself hungry while waiting, now you have to pay the extra tax on the prices just to eat the food in the restaurants at the airport or from the sundry while you wait to board your flight. It seriously hurts my heart to have to pay fifteen dollars for a five-dollar burger. To add insult to injury, I don't know how long I will be in Georgia, so I packed enough clothes for a few weeks. I thought I was going to be required to pay an extra sixty dollars to check my bags but remembered that Southwest doesn't charge you to check your first two bags like the other airlines and, while I recognize that it's all designed to make convenience more expensive, I am not happy with the airport fees and prices. Feeling overwhelmed, I am dreading my visit to Georgia, so everything is bothering me. I pick up the phone and begin to dial my dad's cellphone number until his name pops up on the screen and press it to call him.

"Hey Bay-girl. Are you getting on the plane?"

"Yeah daddy," I say, "I'm getting on the plane shortly. I just wanted you to know that I am already at the airport. I should be landing around 12:30 A.M."

"Ok baby. I will be there with one of your sisters to get you. The other one is going to stay with your mother. Call me as soon as you land."

"Ok daddy."

Without saying "goodbye" my dad hangs up the phone. I close my eyes as I slowly pull the phone away from my face, holding back the tears. I know it's wrong, but I don't want to see the woman who has been everything but a mother to me. I walk slowly through the airport when I see a smoothie shop that reminds me of

EIGHT MOMENTS

Orange Julius. I haven't seen one of those in years. My mom used to take us there for a special treat. But, when things went bad between us, my mom left me in the mall.

We were sitting in the Food Court when I asked her if I could have an *Orange Julius* smoothie. After a brief pause, and forced smile, she handed me three dollars without giving me the opportunity to ask my sisters if they'd wanted one and told me to run along. It kind of made me feel special. My mom was finally doing something nice for me again, like she used to do, and I couldn't have been happier. Her voice was "motherly-firm" as she said, "Come right back to the table." I skipped off to the store, excited about my smoothie and couldn't wait to come back and share it with my sisters. Five minutes seemed like forever as I stood in line, waiting patiently as I made my way towards the cashier. But when I got back to the table where I'd left them only a few minutes prior, they were gone. I spent almost two hours looking for them, crying with a melted smoothie in my hand that I'd

CHAPTER 2

become too upset to drink. The security guard felt bad for me as he walked me around the food court a few times to look for a family that was nowhere to be found. There were no cell phones then, and I was too young to have a pager so there was no way I could contact her. My face had become flushed and I entered panic mode as I burst into a full-blown ugly cry. It was the type of crying that causes uncontrollable facial spasms with saliva dripping down your chin and snot running from your nose. I had several tears falling down my face and stood in the middle of the walkway with my mouth wide open as passersby tried to figure out what was wrong. After the security guard calmed me down ten minutes later, we checked the bathrooms thinking maybe my sisters had to go but she wasn't there as I continued to try to catch my breath from my tearful breakdown. Finally, we walked through the mall, peering in every store and making announcements in every department store for her to come to my rescue. When none of that worked, we walked to the parking lot, to find her sitting in the car, reading a book. She looked up and had the audacity to scold me in front of the officer, making him believe that she'd told me to come straight to the car. "Donna where have you been?" she snapped. The security guard responded on my behalf, "Looking for you?" At that very moment, I got the feeling that he wasn't buying what she was trying to sell until she motioned towards my sisters on the back seat. The sleeping beauties were used as explanation for why she was unable to come inside. The security guard looked at her and said, "Ma'am your daughter has been gone for over two hours, and you didn't think something was wrong?" He was right. I had been looking for her for almost two hours with him, and that is only because he knew me. There is no way a mother in her right mind would have not been frantic. My mother, though, could care less about what I was doing. I shouldn't have been gone for more than fifteen minutes. But that was how my mother treated me, she thrived on the emotional abuse she issued to me, and let me tell you, it was issued to me daily.

CHAPTER 2

I pull my thoughts together as I walk to the gate when I hear the announcement that they are about to board my flight and even though it has been years since my mother left me in the mall, I am still that little girl in the red dress and ponytails, looking for my mother because that's the day I realized I'd truly lost my mother. Little did I know, the worst was yet to come.

"Good evening ladies and gentlemen and welcome to Southwest Airlines flight number 2730 to Atlanta with a final destination to Dallas. We are now boarding passengers who needed special assistance or who are boarding with children. Once again, if you need assistance, or are boarding with children, you may begin boarding at this time. Thank you for choosing Southwest Airlines and have a wonderful day!" The attendant sounded eerily cheerful as she spouted those words and I begin to gather my belongings to get on the flight. I am truly not ready to see my mom. Hell, to be honest, I'm not ready to go back to Georgia. I'm going to honor my father's wish to visit and see what my mother wants. Maybe this time I can take her to the mall so she can get an *Orange Julius* smoothie and leave her there as a reminder of what she did to me. I didn't cause Sam's death. I loved my brother with all of my heart and a piece of me died with him. Why my mother insisted on punishing me for his death is still a mystery. Maybe she wants to talk to me and tell me why she flipped on me and treated me so poorly. It's easy to come to your senses when you are on your death bed. That is when you want to make amends. I remember a story about an inmate, James Washington, who had killed a woman by beating her to death. He was never prosecuted because there was no evidence to link him to the murder. However, while in prison for another crime he'd committed, he had a seizure and decided to confess to a prison guard. I compare him to my mother because she beat me throughout life, mentally and physically. I suffered from her disdain for me and even explored killing myself to make it stop. I no longer wanted to be in a home where my mother

CHAPTER 2

valued my life just as much as the value of Monopoly money; and even that is a stretch in comparison. This woman hates me, and she made sure I was reminded every day I was with her. I remember the amount of disgust and disdain in her eyes, she literally scowled whenever I was in her presence.

"Attention everyone," the stewardess interrupts my thoughts again, "thank you for your patience. We are now boarding passengers with Boarding pass A, seats 1-30. Again, we are now boarding passengers with Boarding pass A, seats one through thirty." I look in the direction of the airline attendant and, seeing the happiness in her eyes and her genuine smile, made me realize that I am definitely not in a good place. I. Do. Not. Want. To. See. My. Mother. I can think of a million other things I can do with my time, my money, and my frequent flyer miles that I cashed in to get here.

It seems like the more I dread this flight, the quicker this damn line moves. I pull my phone out of my purse to shoot Maggie a quick text. "I'm boarding my flight now," I write and quickly press send. I hear a ding on the loud speaker followed by the attendant's voice. "Ladies and gentlemen at this time we will continue boarding Southwest flight number 2730. We are now boarding passengers A, thirty-one to sixty. Passengers with boarding passes B, one through thirty, please go ahead and line up for our next round of seating."

I look down at my boarding pass and read B-30 aloud. I let out a sigh because they aren't quite ready for me yet before I laugh as I realize that's my age so I can't forget it. I nervously reach up to touch the coils of my hair before I begin to type a group message to my sisters. "I'm boarding the plane now. Please tell daddy," the message reads. Sierra quickly responds with a bunch of smiley face emojis to represent her excitement and then Chandler responds with, "I was trying to plan a small family gathering to welcome you back home but mom told me to stop." When will she ever learn? That's typical "mom" behavior when it comes to me. Showing a brave face, and feeling a

CHAPTER 2

twinge of sympathy, I respond with a simple, "Maybe she doesn't want the family to see her like this." Sierra quickly responds with, "Maybe so."

I re-read the brief exchange between myself and my sisters and then go to my call log as they continue to board the flight. I stop at Stephen's number. Should I give him a call? He may be asleep? Will I disturb his daughter by calling this late? I decide against it, click the side button to turn off the screen, and slide the phone in my purse when I look up to see a young girl staring at me. She looked like she may be about five. She smiles at me when she realizes I am looking back at her and bashfully buries her head into her mother's leg. She tries to peek at me again and I smile at her. I wave and she waves back before burying her face again. She has big, brown eyes and a beautiful smile and I begin to wonder if Stephen's daughter resembles her. Her mother looks at her to see who she is hiding from and smiles at me. "I was wondering who she was staring at earlier," she says. I smile and my response is simply, "She probably noticed that I needed a smile. Kids have that sixth sense you know. They can tell when someone needs a brighter day." My phone buzzes and I look down as the mother says, "I guess you're right." A gentleman walks over to her to grab her attention and I open the phone to see who is trying to reach out to me. Surprisingly, its Stephen.

"Hello," I answer.

"Well good evening miss lady," he says cheerfully.

"Good evening. I was just thinking about you," I say, "I figured you'd be asleep so I decided against calling."

"Well, you actually did call me."

"Oh no. I'm so sorry. I must have dialed you when I slid the phone in my purse."

"It's ok Donna. I don't mind. I was waiting to hear from you."

"You were?'

"Yes."

I pause for a moment before I respond but, before I can say anything, he begins speaking.

"You seem worried. Is everything going to be ok?" He asks.

CHAPTER 2

"No."

"Would you like to talk about it?"

"I'm about to board the plane so I'd rather not."

"I see. Well, I'm glad you thought of me and called me, even if it was by accident." I can hear a smile in his voice, similar to when he was talking to his daughter while in the grocery store.

"Are you smiling?" I ask.

"Maybe."

"Well, I was thinking you wouldn't answer and debated calling you because I didn't know if you were asleep."

"I asked you to call me."

"Sure, when I make it to Georgia, not before."

"Donna. I'm glad you called. I can't wait to actually get a chance to really talk to you."

"Trust me, there will be plenty of time for that while I am in Georgia. My family will all be at my mom's beck-and-call so that will give me a lot of free time."

"Won't you also be doing a lot for her?"

EIGHT MOMENTS

"I will do whatever is needed of me." I didn't want to tell him that my mother is a raving lunatic who has attempted to hurt me, and almost kill me, practically all my life. It's too early to share my business with him. My silence, however, speaks volumes and makes the conversation a little awkward. He can tell I am distracted. "Hey Donna. I can tell there is a lot on your mind. Please call me when you land, or at least send a text. Ok?" he asks. "Ok," I say. We hang up the phone and I walk over to my place in line. I regretfully board the plane, get settled, and close my eyes to say a quick prayer.

"Heavenly Father,
Please watch over this plane as we travel to our final destinations. Watch over the pilots and give them wisdom, strength, and the fortitude necessary to do their jobs safely. Father, I pray for my family and ask for strength while visiting Georgia. I need your guidance, and ask you to order my steps and guide my tongue in your son Christ Jesus' name. Amen."

CHAPTER 2

I open my eyes and wait for take-off. I love to see the plane rising into the clouds. It's the reminder I need to keep reaching for the stars. Once we are at a steady altitude, I ask the Flight Attendant for a Bloody Mary and hand her a drink coupon. Aside from the rest I will need so that I won't be consumed by this thing with my mother, I need a stiff drink too.

After gulping down my drink, I grab my neck pillow and lean back now that the wheels are up and I have had a drink to calm my nerves, it's time for me to close my eyes.

EIGHT MOMENTS

-3-

Behind Locked Doors

An evening of traveling is taxing on the body and I just want to relax but I know that my mother is waiting for me. If she is trying to give me an apology for all of the messed-up things she did to me as a child, she can keep it. Why apologize for the abuse now? I certainly don't need it. Is she trying to clear her conscience before she passes away? This woman, who has done everything she can to show me that she doesn't love me, who intentionally made my heart ache after Sam died, can't possibly have enough words, or explanations, for what she has done to me. Besides, it only opens wounds I'd rather keep closed. I look out the window as my father drives. He can tell there is something wrong, and so can my sister, Chandler. Feeling both of their eyes

CHAPTER 3

fixated on me, I ask, "Sierra is with momma, right?" I continue to stare out the window. Daddy responds first, "Yes. She is so excited that you have come home." Chandler adds, "She and momma both have said they can't wait to see you. It's been almost twelve years since you've been home." My dad shoots her a look through the rearview mirror, thinking I wasn't paying attention, and mouthed the words, "Don't mention your mother." I mumble under my breath, "It would have been twelve more if I'd had anything to do with it." I have been perfectly fine in my little bubble in Houston, away from this drama, and didn't want to come back. I certainly didn't want to come back to this. Not now. Chandler and Sierra have always had a problem understanding how I felt when it came to our mother. Chandler is the oldest and is now thirty-two. Sierra is thirty-one. To know them is to love them. Sierra is the hugger and they are the best hugs in the world. She doesn't let go until you pull away. It almost feels as if she is feeding your soul with all the love she has to give with each hug. Growing up, she didn't talk much. She is more of a take-action kind of person and we are a lot alike because we are equally active in the community. Physically, we both took a lot of features from our father. We both have curly afros, hers is slightly bigger than mine, dimples, sun-kissed golden skin, and brown eyes. I got his height at six feet one inch and she is mom's height, at five feet five inches. Thank you for the six feet seven-inch frame family genes gave my daddy. It's one of the things I always loved. Sierra is engaged and has no children. She met her fiancé while volunteering at a nursing home. He was there to see Ms. Lydia, his grandmother. Apparently, the grandmother asked Sierra to come see her at the exact time she'd asked Aaron to bring her some fresh flowers. Of course, the flowers were for my sister, he just didn't know it. A grandmother's wisdom will keep you on your toes. Her only wish now is that they hurry up and marry before she passes away but from what I hear, she is as healthy as a prize-winning ox and not going anywhere any time soon. She lives in the assisted-

CHAPTER 3

living home, as she calls it, so she can be near friends and not bother her grandson to take her places throughout the week. He doesn't mind, however, because she is his only living grandparent and he adores her. Depending on how ill mom is, Sierra may try to have the wedding while I'm home.

Chandler, on the other hand, looks just like mom and has always been very chatty. She is the one who will say whatever is on her mind, and doesn't always think before she speaks. Her husband, Chad, is a very patient and loving man. Quiet, he is pretty laid back and allows her to be herself. They have been married for five years and have two children, her son Chance, and Chandler, her daughter whom she, of course, named after herself. Her daughter is literally her twin. I can always count on her saying too much when it isn't necessary, and bringing up my mother because she wants us to mend our relationship. She says her kids need their auntie in their lives because they always ask about me. Her light skin tone always turns flush when she is frustrated with me about anything dealing with mom. She, too, has dad's dimples and they show all the time, even when she isn't trying. But, she has brown eyes and her curls are a little looser than ours with a petite shape. She is only five feet tall but she has a big personality.

As we approach the house, I think about the day I left for college, when my mother wouldn't even come out to say goodbye. Couple that with the fact that she was always too busy for my weekly Friday check-ins, telling me she was too busy to talk and it made me say that I would never come back to see her but, somehow, here I am. The house still looks the same after all of these years. A blue house with white trim. The long driveway lined with perfectly manicured shrubs made for a big yard. As my father grabs my bags out of the trunk, I walk to the door, feeling my feet become heavier with each step. Chandler pulls out her keys and fumbles until she's able to open the door. Funny, I never had a key. I always had to wait to be let in and locked out. My dad tried to sneak a key to me but my mom

CHAPTER 3

saw him fumbling with my keyring and
took it back before I could even see it the
next morning. When I asked him to lock
the door as I headed out for work, he was
baffled about the key's whereabouts until
momma walked in and told him she took it
because, "that heffa isn't responsible
enough for a key." At least that is how she
put it. Meanwhile, everyone else seemed
to be responsible enough, even Sierra who
lost her keys every other month. I follow
Chandler into the house and am greeted by
some good old-fashioned soul food aroma
coming from the kitchen. I can smell the
collard greens and cornbread and I smile
because I know my daddy did all of this for
me. He walks in behind me and tells me
that he is taking my bags to my old room.
"Your mother didn't change it after you
left," he says, his voice trailing behind him
as he walks away. I look at him curiously
and then Chandler shrugs. Several
thoughts are running through my mind,
like, it's late as hell so I can't eat all this
heavy food right now. As if Chandler is
reading my mind, she says, "You are going
to have to eat something or his feelings

will be hurt." "Thanks for making me feel guilty Chandler," I say. In twelve years, and after several visits to my house, no one bothered to share that little detail with me. Aside from the fact that it's strange that she never changed my room, I wonder what else *hasn't* changed. I'm starting to feel overwhelmed and I grab my phone. I send text messages to Maggie and JoAnn, respectively to let them know I made it safely. Finally, I call Stephen and as the phone is ringing, Chandler grabs my hand and pulls me to my parent's room, announcing that I am finally home. Stephen answers groggily and I tell him I made it safely. "Go back to sleep. We will talk later," I say.

There she is, Mrs. Dianne Catchings, my mother. When she realizes I'm at the door, Sierra runs towards me with a bright smile, but there is a sadness in her eyes. She hugs me tight and doesn't let go for at least a minute. My mother is in the bed, trying to sit up. Her eyes light up when she sees me, something I haven't seen since before Sam died, and even then, I don't remember them lighting up when

CHAPTER 3

she saw me. My father walks in and kisses her on her forehead. He whispers to her that I am home and he is glad that he finally got his family back together. Watching this scene breaks my heart, mainly because Sam can't be here. Tears begin to form in my eyes and, as if she knows why I am crying, my mother says through staggered breaths, "Sam's death wa-a-sn't your f-f-fault." I walk over to her and she reaches out for a hug. Reluctantly, I hug her back. She kisses my cheek and motions for me to sit in the chair beside her while shooing everyone else out of the room. Everybody leaves in ushered silence and my father looks at us once more before closing the door. I begin to panic. Why is he closing me up in this room with this psychotic woman? I glance across the room, surprised that no one took the pillows out for fear that I may suffocate her. Then again, they know I would never do anything to physically harm her. I can't say that I haven't thought about it though. My mother looks at me and says, "I know y-y-you're wondering why I-I wanted to talk to you in p-p-person." She winces in pain. I stand up to help her get comfortable in the bed but don't say a word. I walk over to the window and look over the back yard. There were so many nights I had to walk in the back yard to get one of my sisters to let me in the house because my mother wouldn't open the door. "Do you remember that?" I ask her. I turned to look at her, knowing she'd be puzzled by my random question.

"Yes." She says and points towards her jewelry box. I pick it up and hand it to her and sit back down. After a few moments of rambling, she pulls out a key and hands it to me. Maybe she knew what I was talking about after all, she watched me in that window enough nights. I take the key and ask, "Why did you want to see me mother?"

"I wanted to say w-w-what I said. S-s-sam's death wasn't your f-f-fault."

"So you didn't want to…" I cut myself off before I could ask for an apology from her; the apology I thought I didn't want.

CHAPTER 3

"I was wrong Donna." I lean in to kiss my mother, the woman who has mistreated me all these years and for the next several moments, there is just silence as she holds my hand. Her hands are cold and her body is frail. She seems weak, like there is no fight left in her. My father knocks on the door and brings in a warm blanket for her that he'd just taken out of the dryer. "It's important to keep her warm Donna," he says, "Are you alright?" I look at him and smile.

"I'm alright daddy."

"Did you all have a good talk?"

"We did." Noticing that my mother had drifted off to sleep, I open my hand to show him the key and ask, "What is this?"

"Your key to the house."

"Oh, I see."

"Everything is not what it seems Donna. Everything is not what it seems."

"I thought she was going to hospice dad. Why is she home?"

"There is nothing they can do for her. They only gave her a few days to live. They figured she would be more comfortable at home with her loved-ones and they said they can give her more attention here."

"What type of cancer is it?"

He looks at me wearily and says, "Liver. It's liver cancer. I noticed that she was losing weight and her stomach was distended but thought she was just eating bad. I had no idea she was drinking as much as she was. She kept complaining that her left shoulder was hurting but the doctor kept telling us nothing was wrong and put her on a special diet."

"How many times did you go to the doctor?"

"Three. It wasn't until she started coughing up blood that they took additional tests at the Emergency Room and, by then, it was already advanced."

I sit down in the chair beside me and rub my hand over my face as I let out a deep sigh. "They didn't think it was cirrhosis? It seems like that would have prompted them to do some checks." I look at my father for a response, but he just stares out the window.

"Dad?"

CHAPTER 3

"Yeah Bay-girl?"

"They didn't think it was cirrhosis?"

"No. They didn't. I kept telling them that she was losing her appetite, that she was experiencing these pains." His eyes start to swell and he begins to cry. "I drove her to drink," he says. This is my fault.

"No one put a bottle in her hand. No one." After a few moments I say, "I'm going to grab a bite to eat. Are you hungry daddy?"

His broken voice lightly whispers, "No." My heart begins to break for him. This man sacrificed all of himself for her, to keep her happy, even at the expense of his own. Now, she is passing away before his eyes and there is nothing he can do about it. What's worse is that he is blaming himself for it. I watch him and wonder why he allowed her to treat me so badly. Why does he think her drinking is his fault? My mother loves him. She looks at him in a way that she has never looked at anyone else. You can see her light up whenever he enters the room. I remember watching them as a child, how they used to playfully tease each other. He has always protected her, covered her when she is cold, held her hand as if he is trying to reassure her that she is the only woman for him. I have always wanted that for myself and I am baffled that this loving man loves her so blindly that he allows her to mistreat a child. I look in his eyes and ask him.

"Daddy. Why did you never say anything to mom? Why did you let her treat me so badly?" He opens his mouth to respond but quickly closes it, looking away.

I guess I knew he wasn't going to answer the question when I asked it. But I wanted to ask anyway. Watching what this death is doing to the family is crushing and now I need to know. Just as I am beginning to ask again, Chandler and Sierra walk into the room. Dammit.

-4-

Death of Sam

"Shut up! Shut up bitch or I will fucking kill you! You better put every bill in the register in the bag." He says to the cashier at the convenience store. I am frozen, looking around for cover, trying to be invisible in an aisle full of old potato chips, candy, and sour pickles. I close my eyes, hoping that will make me undetectable. The cashier whimpers as she nervously tries to place the money in the bag. "I don't have anything over twenty dollars," she whimpers.

"Bitch, I didn't ask you about that. Did I?" The robber screams as he waves the gun. "Put the damn money in the bag before I blow your head off!" I look around for Sam and point to the back-exit door as he slowly shakes his head to tell me no. He mouths the words, "Stay put!" I nod at him in agreement. I'm terrified and look over to see one of the robbers heading towards me. What am I going to do?! Oh no. Oh no. "Hey," the guy says to me, "Get your little ass over here and sit on the floor. Empty out your pockets while you're at it." He points the gun at me to let me know he means business so I walk towards him at a snail's pace, trying not to look at Sam, who is hiding behind an endcap and out of the line of sight of the mirrors. "Hurry up 'lil girl before I pop a cap in your ass and stop all that crying!" He says as Sam goes unnoticed. I wipe my face with my sleeve and try to stay calm, sit on the floor, and empty out my pockets. I only had two dollars and forty-seven cents, all of which I hand to him. He grabs it and walks away.

"Hey!" The third robber calls out. "Who are you in here with?" He walks over to me but I remain silent while looking down at the floor; trying to avoid eye contact. "Did you hear me?" He asked. I look at him and stutter, "N-n-nobody." As he continues to walk towards me, another customer walks into the store and he turns towards him and opens fire, shooting him in the chest. I gasp and the

CHAPTER 4

cashier screams. Sam has made his way closer to me and motions for me to move closer to him while the robbers begin to argue.

The one holding the cashier at gunpoint says, "Nigga is you crazy? What the fuck did you shoot that man for? We gotta get outta here before the police come." The cashier continues to scream as he says, "Bitch I told yo ass to shut the fuck up." He then shoots her in the head at point-blank range. Blood and brain matter splatters everywhere and Sam begins to run towards me to keep me from the crossfire when the second robber opens fire on him. Three shots. It all seems to happen in slow motion as one bullet hits him in the chest, the second in the shoulder, and the third in the head. His mouth was open because he was trying to yell at me to stay close to him when the third shot rang out and he landed on top of me.

I wake up in a cold-sweat and my body is feeling heavy, like Sam's body is still on top of me. I smell banana candy so I know my mind is playing tricks on me.

EIGHT MOMENTS

Banana flavored Laffy Taffy was Sam's favorite candy and it was what he smelled like when he fell on me the day he died. I lay in the bed, breathing heavy, blinking to make sure I was just dreaming and whisper, "I miss you Sam." I look over at and see a figure standing by the window. I can't make out any distinctive features, I just see red shoes with blue trim, the shoes Sam's killer was wearing as he walked over to shoot me to make sure they left no witnesses behind. I sit up and shake my head, my heart is racing as I glance at the corner again. I shouldn't have eaten so heavy before going to bed because my mind is all over the place. I slide the covers off of me and throw my legs over the bed, my toes dangling just enough to search for refuge in my slippers because I need a little fresh air and some water. I look around my room. Sierra and Chandler were right, mom didn't change a thing and everything I left was still in the same place. But, I don't take this as a sign of love, just a closed admission of guilt. Or, maybe she didn't go in my room because ignoring it is a part of the façade

CHAPTER 4

she uses to act like something, or someone, doesn't exist. Maybe I was supposed to be a boy too and she would have had two boys and two girls, a perfect family. I slide on the housecoat that I'd laid at the foot of the bed last night and walk towards the kitchen to make myself a glass of water and I see my phone sitting on the counter. I guess I must have put it down as I was taking my luggage to my room after my father and I ate. I pick it up and scroll through to see that JoAnn and Stephen sent text messages. Stephen was asleep when I called to tell him I'd made it and JoAnn was shocked that I was in Georgia. I decide to wait until later to respond to them. I slide the phone in my housecoat's pocket and walk to the cabinet to grab a glass and stand there for a few seconds before walking to the refrigerator to get some water. I can't get the Laffy Taffy smell out of my nose and I begin to cry. Being back in this house is hard for me and I am having memories that I don't want to remember, incidents that really took a piece of my innocence with them. Sam's death shook our family hard but it broke my mom more than anything and in turn, she decided to break me. I finish drinking my water and put the glass in the sink before I walk into the Living Room and am startled by a sudden movement and then the light comes on. It's my father. Startled, I ask, "What are you doing up?" I walk closer to him and see that his eyes are puffy and red. He's been crying and worried about mom. He picks up a glass of Jameson and begins to drink. His words are heavy as he drunkenly mumbles, "Are you okay Bay-girl? I uh, I heard you talking in your sleep." He looks at me carefully, like he is trying to see what I am thinking and I don't know how to respond to him. I candidly say, "Coming back here is making me revisit memories I thought I'd dealt with, or at least buried away." I grab a blanket off the couch and sit down on the floor in front of his chair. Together we sit in silence until he pours another drink and hands me a glass. He rubs the top of my head and says, "I heard your mother tell you that it wasn't your fault. She wasn't talking about Sam." He takes a sigh and says, "I should have done a better

CHAPTER 4

job of protecting you. Just know I love you baby." I sit in silence for a moment because the impact of his words hit me harder than a ton of bricks. You're damn right you should have protected me. You should have found out why she was treating me so differently. I mean, there were several nights that I heard them arguing about me, I have heard him say that she needed to calm down and let it go, that he loves all of his children and treats us all the same and so should she. But, he never defended me. I was just a child who had gone through something tragic and my mother never gave me a chance to heal. "Daddy," I call out after a few moments of thinking but he doesn't answer. I turn around to see him sleeping peacefully, still holding his glass. I watch as his chest moves back and forth at a rhythmic pace before I grab his glass and remove his glasses. I have so many questions that need answers. I feel like a puzzle that needs to be put together and I don't like the feeling. I am used to being in control and removing anything out of my life that doesn't serve a purpose. But you can't do that with family, and it seems natural selection has decided to take my mom before she can really dig into the root of the problems she has. I laugh at myself. I can't believe that I have so callously shelved her death as natural selection. I should be ashamed and if I don't get my attitude together, I am no better than her. I shake my head to snap out of it and stand up, covering my father with the blanket. He probably hasn't slept like this in days and he needs his rest because it is only going to get worse. I lean over and kiss him on his forehead, realizing that I am not angry with him. I only want answers. My father has always shown me how much he loves me, sometimes more than my sisters. Maybe he has been trying to compensate for my mother all of these years. Or, it could be that he has been trying to make up for all of those times that she treated me like I wasn't a part of the family. Either way, this woman has never had very much love for me.

I won't be able to get any sleep after this so I decide to check my work email. It's a good thing that they come to my cell phone because I don't feel like grabbing the computer. Melanie's name is the first to pop up. Her email is routine, make sure you enter customer follow up information in the system. She sent another email asking if I'd made it safely and told me to take a few days off. I guess she sensed the urgency in my issue. I respond and tell her that my mother is under hospice care. That is enough information to tell her that it is serious without telling her what it is, or how serious it is. Its none of her business. I can't stand her anyway. I continue to sift through emails and am thankful that my remaining conference call for the week has been cancelled, when a text message pops up. It's JoAnn who asks, "How are you holding up?"

"I'm good." I respond.

"Are you?" She asks.

"Yes. Call me." I respond.

"No."

"Why not? You know I need you to help me sort through my mom's words to understand what she means."

EIGHT MOMENTS

"Because I am not your mother. I can't speak for her. You are right there with her. Talk to her."

"What?"

She doesn't respond to my last text so I send, "JoAnn???" Again, no response. I know what she is trying to do but I can't help but feel like she is abandoning me and I can't stand it. I want to throw the phone across the room but don't want to tear it up so I slide in back in my pocket, grab the bottle of Jameson and glass, and shuffle towards my room.

As I pass my parent's room, I hear a loud humming noise. It must be one of the machines they have connected to her. I stand by the door for a few minutes, not wanting to go inside, listening to the whir of the machine until it suddenly seems like the humming is close to me and I realize that my phone is vibrating in my pocket. Maybe that is why it seems so loud. I look at the phone to see it is Melanie so I hurry to my room and close the door before answering.

"Hello Melanie."

CHAPTER 4

"Donna, you didn't tell me that it was this serious." She almost sound concerned. And what's with her calling me Donna? That's new. She has always called me Ms. Catch-ings. "I can handle it." I say and she asks, "Donna, what's wrong?" There it is, the dreaded question. "Nothing Mela…" She cuts me off, "Donna, I know we don't have a close relationship, but this is serious. How bad is it?" "It's bad." I hold my ground, determined to keep my family business to myself and she can see right through it. "You know, when my daughter was in the hospital, I was like you. I didn't want to tell anyone how bad it really was. I didn't want to have too many people in my business and I certainly didn't want to hear all of the sympathy from people who didn't really mean it or care. But, I realized that it was not my burden to bear alone and I had to keep my boss informed if I wanted to keep my job." There she is, the old Melanie subtly threatening my job came back in full force. I knew it wouldn't take long but she has a point. I have to tell her what is going on so I can take some time to deal with all of this. "My mother is dying and only has a few weeks to live per the doctors. She has cancer." I hear Melanie gasp. It is the first time I have ever known her to be speechless. "Are you serious?" She asks but answers her own question by saying, "Of course you're serious. I've never known you to lie about anything, especially something so devastatingly close." Her words come as a surprise. It's good to know that she doesn't think I'm a liar but now it makes me wonder why the hell she accused me of lying to her the other day, when she heard from the four people she could *trust*. I guess that was just a ploy to ruffle my feathers. She *is* known to do that from time to time. "Melanie, I'll be fine. Please, let's just keep this between us." I plead. "Donna, I know that this is rough and I cannot, in good conscience, allow you to work like this when you should be with your mom. I will tell Tom that he will be the primary on your accounts for the next few weeks and that you have something personal that came up. Don't worry about joining any conference calls, I will handle that and send you the notes. All I ask is that you check your emails and respond each day and keep me posted and if it gets too heavy for you, let me know. I'll call you next week. Ok?" after a brief pause I say, "Ok Melanie. I will talk to you later." She hangs up the phone after saying, "I'll be in touch."

The conversation with Melanie was not what I expected at all. Interesting. I suddenly don't have a taste for the liquor anymore and I just want to rest. I sit the glass and bottle on the nightstand, take off my robe, and climb into bed. God, please let me be able to sleep without incident. I pray for a good night's rest but falling back asleep is becoming a difficult task. I toss and turn for a little while until I hear a light buzz and grab my phone out of my housecoat pocket. "Have a nice day Ms. Lady. Call me when you get a chance." It's a text message from Stephen which, surprisingly, makes me smile. It's been awhile since I have been pursued by a man but I don't know if I am ready to entangle him in this mess of a life I have right now. Still, I pick up the phone and call him,

EIGHT MOMENTS

"Well good morning Ms. Lady." I can tell he is smiling through his words. "Hello Stephen," I say. I begin to smile too, feeling a rush of happiness jump through my chest like a kid jumping through the clouds, building sandcastles in the sky and riding on rainbows. Conversation with him is easy, comfortable. "How are you holding up Donna?" He asks.

"Let's see. I just made it here early this morning and in a matter of hours, I have managed to talk to my mother who brought up a few painful moments and had a vivid dream about my big brother's death. I can only imagine what's next."

"I know we just met but I can definitely be your shoulder if you need to cry, or your listening ear, if you need to vent. I'd love to get to know you." His words seem so genuine and heartfelt which makes my smile fade. How can I let him get to know me when I am starting to realize that I don't even know myself? I start to panic and try to figure out a way to get off the phone when Sierra walks into the room calling my name. "Thank you, God, for sending her to my rescue," I say

CHAPTER 4

in silent prayer. "Ummm Stephen. I need to call you back." "Ok. Think about what I said and keep your head up. Talk to you later." I disconnect the call after saying, "Ok I will. I'll call you later."

"What's up?" I ask Sierra. "Everything ok?" I look in her face and see worry lines and solemn eyes. Sierra can see mom slipping away and it is taking a toll on her. She has always been sensitive. Her brown eyes dart away from me to the window and down to the floor before she decides to respond. "I am worried that you and mom won't make amends before she dies. I haven't been able to sleep all night and I knew you were awake. Actually, everyone in the house is awake except for dad." I responded, "He hasn't been asleep for long and, from the looks of it, he needs it."

From the looks of it, everyone needs rest. Sierra went on and on about how my father keeps talking about how he worried mom to her death bed and he feels responsible. "Feels responsible?" I question her. That statement puzzles me. Why would my dad think that he is the reason my mother has cancer? He had just told me earlier that he was the one who drove her to drink. I look at Sierra, "When did mom start drinking?" I ask. "She started drinking after Sam died but no one knew it. Dad was trying to hide it." "After Sam died?" I repeat and put my head in my hands. Shit. I never knew she was drinking but it explains some of her behavior. I was nine when Sam died but, in fear, I told everyone I was twelve so the robbers wouldn't find me if they'd started looking, at least that was my juvenile train of thought. I saw each of their faces and I knew they'd be after me. The lie I told was a defense mechanism but it didn't help that momma introduced me to Red Shoes the day after the murder and when she heard me say I was twelve, she snatched me up quickly calling me a "little fast-ass girl." Sam was only fifteen and risked his life to save mine and mom couldn't handle it. She always talked about how much she'd wanted a boy before she had Sam. He was her baby. So, I can see how she could have started drinking under the radar. A drink here and there to sleep and then one

CHAPTER 4

to cope until it became a daily habit she just couldn't, or wouldn't, quit. I try to take Sierra's mind off of mom's death but only make it worse when I mention the wedding. "Have you and Aaron set a date yet?" I ask her. "We haven't decided. I thought mom would get better but she is only getting worse. We may just have a small ceremony here in the back yard next weekend. The whole family is kind of on stand-by since mom fell ill." Her words are shaky as she forces out another sentiment, "Yeah. I think mom will like that. Will you uh, will you help me plan and decorate it? I know you are good at that sort of thing." I grab her hand and smile at her, "I will be happy to help you." She hugs me tightly and doesn't let go for a long time. I can hear her sniffling and know that she is crying for our mother. It saddens me that I don't have those same tears. I tried for years to maintain a relationship with her, called her every Friday, only to be treated like a second thought. She was always too busy to talk to me. I was always bothering her. I close my eyes to try to think of the good times but nothing comes to mind, at least not after Sam's death. Even before he died, she wasn't the most pleasant, but she did act like she loved me. She was hard on me, disciplined me. She made sure I spoke well, I was dressed well, and that I was respectful to my elders. She made sure I was fed and never let anyone *else* mistreat me. But, it stopped there. She was never affectionate towards me. She never called me into a big, warm hug or gave me motherly advice. She merely just made sure that I didn't embarrass her and, since there were four of us, it was easy to ignore me and get away with it. But I was always the explorer, the one who didn't mind trying new things. I wanted to learn the world around me and I would talk to anyone who would listen. She never cared because it meant she didn't have to talk to me or put forth any effort to engage me. When I got a little older and asked her to drop me off at the library, that was right up her alley. She would leave me there all day and take everyone else shopping, or out for treats. Some of her friends probably thought I either didn't exist, or I was a

CHAPTER 4

daddy's girl, and that was perfectly ok with me because I was. My daddy had me wrapped around his finger and I preferred to stay with him than go somewhere with momma any day of the week. It would break my heart when he would make me leave him to go with her.

I pull away from Sierra as I search for words to share with her but I am literally drawing a blank. I can't tell her that momma is going to be ok. She isn't. I can't even tell her that I know how she feels because I don't and, to be honest, I don't want to know. I don't want to be buried in grief. So I look her in the eyes and tell her, "We will make your wedding special, something mom will love and you will never forget." I kiss her on the cheek and ask, "Ok?" She shakes her head and says, "Yes." "Good. Let's go check on her and make sure she doesn't need anything and then we can get started." I say before standing up. I probably won't be able to fall asleep again anyway. Maybe taking care of mom will help me take my mind off of things. I grab my toiletry bag and head towards the bathroom to brush my teeth and wash my face then head towards my parent's bedroom. The whirring sound of her machine starts to buzz again as I get closer. I lightly knock on the door and her nurse opens it and motions for me to enter. "Hi mom," I say. I feel someone touch my arm and realize that it is Sierra. She walks over to mom and brushes her hair out of her face. Mom never takes her eyes off of me which makes me uncomfortable. She whispers, "You're so beautiful." I look behind me to see if Chandler walked in and she laughed. "I was talking to you Donna." Did I just step into the twilight zone? She is usually meaner than a snake ready to attack when it comes to me. Her words are always venomous. This *new* mom I am encountering is taking me for a loop but I manage to find the words, "Thank you mom," while saying them as sincerely as possible. Trying to change the mood of the room, I say, "Sierra has something she wants to say to you." Sierra shoots me a look of confusion and I discreetly point to the ring finger on my hand. "Mom," she says, "Aaron and I are going to have the wedding in the back yard next week. We have been talking about it, the family is on standby, and Donna agreed to help me pull it all together. What do you think? Do you think you will be up to it?" My mom smiles but I see a glimpse of sadness in her eyes. She whispers that she loves the idea and asks her what her colors will be. Mom's favorite colors are coral and aqua blue. It's spring here so those colors will work if Sierra decides to pay homage to her and use those colors. We could make it very tropical and beautiful. Sierra tells her that she will have to ask Aaron what colors he has in mind and then turns giddy, knowing that everyone will be at her wedding but I see something in mom that tells me she won't be around much longer.

-5-

The Accident

As Sierra's wedding plans are under way, I worry about how much time we really have before mom is unable to attend. Her health is visibly fading fast. Sierra decided that she wants her colors to be aqua, green and yellow. I immediately get to work on coming up with a garden wedding scheme and decide it would be a good idea to get a tent in case of rain, plus mom would do better in a climate-controlled environment. It's a good thing that my parents have a big back yard, and Sierra has a pretty big budget. She has been saving for her dream wedding for over eight years. I can create a perfect wedding for her and she will still have enough money left to have a fantastic honeymoon and a down payment for a house. I walk to my mom's room to try to get her input, and see if she has any contacts for last minute flowers, dresses, and a cake. Mom knows a lot of people, and they adore her, so I know she can be of assistance. It will also give us time to continue talking, maybe even relieve some of the tension I still feel when I walk in the room. Sierra has given me the reigns saying, "You're always calm in stressful situations. I know you will be able to plan this because I am a wreck." She knows that I want the best for her and will stay up every night if I need to in order to pull this off. She and Aaron have already handled the invitations. Together, they hand delivered them to about fifty people who are guaranteed to come. I'm sure they are going to bring guests. So is Sierra. To be on the safe side, I will plan for a hundred and fifty people, to include plates for the vendors. "Mom, what do you think about this dress?" I show her a picture of a dress I can pick up for her to wear to the wedding. It's a beautiful silver colored gown with beading along the neckline. She seems to perk up when she realizes that I am helping with the wedding planning. "You always were a great event planner and I've heard about the rallies you've been organizing," she says, "I like that dress very much." Not knowing how to respond, I say, "Ok. I looked at it this morning and thought it'd be nice for you so I put it on hold. I will go get it this afternoon." She begins to cough uncontrollably so I grab her water and offer it to her to drink. "Do you need anything?" I ask. "No. This is fine. L-l-et's talk about the wedding." I look in her eyes and can see that she needs this, to feel like she is a big part of this wedding, so I oblige her. "Mom can you give me the names of a baker and florist? Is Ms. Sherry still in business?" She shakes her head yes and then tells me to contact Linda at *For Goodness Cakes* in Norcross.

"Sierra. Can you come in here for a second?" I call out.

"What's up?" She asks as she enters the room.

"I need to make sure that you are ok with my idea. Since we have a short period of time, I was thinking we could get one tier with sugar flowers and just add fresh flowers on the top of cupcakes. The cupcakes can be replenished as they dwindle and you can take the top tier to freeze for your first anniversary. Is that okay with you?"

"I never thought of that," she says.

"What flavor do you like? Champagne? Chocolate? White Chocolate? Vanilla bean? They even have an Orange Velvet cake on their website. Have you had their cakes before? They have really good reviews and mom suggested them. I figure you'd know which flavor you like best." She looks at mom and asks, "What do you think mom?" Mom responds, "Vanilla bean and white chocolate." She smiles at Sierra and then looks at me saying, "Good idea Donna." Sierra agrees. "Then it's settled. I will give them a call in a few minutes." I say.

"I already have a caterer," Sierra says, "They are going to be there early Saturday to set up and will have a staff there to serve. Aaron's cousin has a catering business and he signed a contract with them today."

"Great. What about a photographer and videographer?" I ask. "Do you have one?"

"No."

"There is a photographer from Mississippi that I know a lot of people rave about. I think his name is Sterling. I have seen some of his work and it is gorgeous. But I think he is pricey." I look him up online and find a number to call his office. I walk out of the room to tell them the situation and our needs. Luckily, he's just had a cancellation for Saturday and agreed to come. "Great. I look forward to receiving the contract and we will send over the deposit once we review it. Thank you so much." I look up to see Sierra smiling at me. "Is he going to do it?" She asks.

"Yes. But it's going to cost you."

"How much?"

"Five thousand. But he will be here all day, will make sure to get a lot of pictures of you and mom, and he is going to throw in the videographer for free because of mom's situation."

"Really?"

CHAPTER 5

"Really."

"That was nice of him to do. Ok. I already have my dress, a make-up artist, and I ordered the linen months ago, I ordered a beautiful personalized runner and table cards. What's next?"

"An officiant."

"We have one. Aaron's uncle is our pastor and he has already given us marriage counseling. He is going to do the wedding." A lot of thoughts rush through my mind and I start to ramble off her wedding needs, "I have to call the florist, we need bridesmaid's dresses and I think the groomsmen will look nice in dark gray suits. We need to rent the tent and then get decorations, a DJ and we need to invite the neighbors so they won't complain about the noise. You already have the rings, I assume?"

"Yes, we have the rings. Don't worry about the DJ either. Aaron took care of that. He got us a band and a DJ. He also made arrangements for all the guys to meet him at his tailor's shop to pick out something to wear so he can pay for it. I will text him your suggestion about the color."

"Awesome. It looks like I just got the contract from Sterling so take a look at it, sign it electronically, send it back, and pay the deposit. I am going to call Ms. Sherry about the flowers to see what she can do. How many bridesmaids and groomsmen do you have?"

"Two. You and Chandler. Little Chan will be my flower girl and Chase is the ring bearer. Aaron's two brothers will be your escorts and Chad will be an usher to make sure everything is going smoothly since the rest of the family will be in the wedding."

"Sounds like you have it all planned."

"No. I couldn't have pulled this together without you. I am so glad you're here." She hugs me tightly and then walks into mom's room with my computer to look over the contract. She sends me a text message with Ms. Sherry's number. Mom must have given it to her.

I call Ms. Sherry and, to my surprise, she remembered me. "How is your mother?" she asks. Not wanting to go into it, I tell her that she is trying to pull through but Ms. Sherry is not concerned with my words. She knows something is wrong. She can feel it. "Tell you what," she says, "I will come by and survey the yard to see how many flowers you need." I don't know what that will solve, we are going to have a tent so I politely decline. "Ms. Sherry, we are going to have a tent in the back yard for the wedding. We don't need a whole lot of flowers. I was thinking about a beautiful arch, two big vases for the wedding party table, and some table arrangements. We will probably need about 20 of those. We also need 5 boutonnieres and two single flower bouquets for the bridesmaids. Sierra already has her bouquet." Sierra got a custom-made brooch bouquet made months ago and, though it cost her a small fortune. It's beautiful. The good thing about this whole thing is that I am not trying to do everything from scratch. The tent people are going to set up and tear down. They are bringing the tables, chairs, and lighted dance floor. Sierra already has the linens ordered and everything else is falling in place. The only thing I have left to do is help her choose the bridesmaids dresses and get daddy's suit. Ms. Sherry wants to contribute more, but her main concern is to be a bit nosy so she agrees to also give Sierra a flower wall for pictures. As a surprise wedding gift, I order some nice wedding party favors, tiny silver foil wrapped champagne bottles, and hire a bartender for an open bar. I need to head to the art supply store to get some items to make a custom board for her and pick up mom's dress. I walk around the house to find daddy in the living room again, sitting in his chair. He avoids eye contact with me. I stand directly in front of him. "Daddy will you be ok if Sierra and I left to run a few errands for the wedding? Nurse Petar is here and Chandler will be here in a few hours." He doesn't answer. "Daddy?" I touch him and he says, "Yes. Go ahead."

"Are you sure?"

"Yes. Go ahead baby. I'll be fine."

I head towards my parent's room and tell Sierra that dad is okay with our plans and then go to my room to change

CHAPTER 5

clothes. It's a good thing that I'm here. I am enjoying helping my sister with her wedding. Everything is coming together.

Sierra drives because she knows that I don't know how to get around anymore. Things have changed. I know how to get home, maybe to the mall and a few other places that I frequented as a child. The place looks different now, though. It's starting to develop and with development, comes new people, places, and things. We ride in silence until we pass a sign which signals our exit to Lake Lanier and I think about the Thompson bridge, and the car accident that almost took my life, my second brush with death. God definitely has something special planned for me because He keeps me here. I close my eyes and I remember the loud boom, the screeching sound of the tires, and the tumble as the car rolled over and over again.

"That's the spot," Sierra says.

"What?" I asked.

"That's where you had the car accident. I was scared as hell when we got the call that you were hurt and being taken to the hospital. The car was totaled."

"Yeah. It's a wonder that I survived."

"It is. You are definitely on this earth to serve a purpose lady." I really don't want to talk about the accident and she can tell. It was a painful experience. I went through months of recovery but was thankful I didn't have to learn how to walk again. My car looked like it was a tuna can.

My daddy and Chandler were the first on the scene and followed the ambulance to the hospital, afraid that I was going to be paralyzed. Chandler called Sierra and my mom who came to the hospital after I had been there for a few hours. Mom said there was no sense in everybody being there worrying about me so she clearly thought it wasn't as serious as it was; until it was, that is. Daddy didn't tell her that the car was totaled he showed her a few pictures he took with his digital camera but her concern wasn't for me, or the fact that the car was gone. Her concern was about the insurance.

CHAPTER 5

"Gabe, did you have Donna's car on insurance?" She asked.

"Yes. She has full coverage."

"Ok. I will contact them and report the accident and I guess I need to contact a lawyer."

When mom found out that I was hit by a drunk driver, a trust-fund baby to be exact, all she saw was dollar signs. That is what I became to her. Days had gone by between her hospital visits, and she just wrote it off to being a mother with two other daughters to care for while I was laid up, getting pampered. After my release, she didn't try to accommodate me to make me comfortable. I think I even remember her telling me to get my ass in the car a time or two because I was moving too slow. She said I needed tough love to get through this tragedy as she ushered me to a few doctor's appointments and therapy sessions. Her goal was to get records and receipts, all of which she gave to the attorney. When everything was said and done, and the lawyer took their cut, I had a nice little settlement to pay for my hospital bills and therapy. It wasn't until bill collectors started calling the house that my father found out that none of the bills had been paid.

"What happened to Donna's settlement money?" He asked her.

"I don't know what you are talking about." She said.

"You know exactly what I'm talking about Dianne!" My father rarely used her name in conversation. He called her pet names like "Baby Cakes", or "Suga," but I'd only heard him call her government name a handful of times. My mother finally conceded, taking him to a closet of brand new handbags, shoes, and clothes. She'd given out loans to her friends and family, and started her business. She also said she paid off the house.

"You paid off the house? How could you do all of this without Donna's signature and where are the house payments I have been giving you to pay the mortgage?" He asked.

"She's a minor and I had Power of Attorney. I didn't need her signature."

CHAPTER 5

It was the first time I'd ever seen my father angry. He stormed out the door and was gone for a couple of hours, returning when he felt like everyone was asleep. But, mom was waiting for him. Sierra told me she heard them arguing. She said he again asked her what the hell she was doing with the mortgage money he'd been giving her for the house to which she answered that she'd been living and supporting her business. Mom had been using the money for months without anyone's knowledge, and by the time he'd caught it, the money was almost gone. There was enough left to pay off the hospital and he disputed the credit reports to make sure I didn't start life off with bad credit because my mother didn't give a damn about it. He was furious with her and slept on the couch for a couple of months while she worked her magic to win him back. After that, mom never handled the finances again. Mom had spent over five hundred thousand dollars when it was all said and done. Dad made her take back all of the new items she hadn't used and he put the money up for me in a trust fund account. For about ten years, he started putting some of the amount he would have been paying for mortgage, about nine hundred dollars a month, into the trust fund. I can't touch it until I'm 35. I never got an apology from my mom for that.

Sierra can tell that talking to me about the accident struck a nerve, so she tries to change the subject by asking, "What color do you think the bridesmaid's dresses should be?"

"I'm not sure Sierra. You chose aqua, green, and yellow for your wedding colors. Maybe Chandler should wear aqua. It will go well with her skin tone and Little Chan and I can wear green. She can throw yellow petals."

"No. I want you and Chandler to wear the same color."

"Yes. But your Matron-of Honor should wear a different color."

"She's my Matron-of-Honor, but you are my Maid-of-Honor and I want you all to have on the same color."

"Ok. We will wear aqua and carry a single yellow rose."

CHAPTER 5

"No. I want you all to have full bouquets."

"Ok. I will send Ms. Sherry an email about the changes and ask her to give us a yellow rose bouquet. Will that work?"

"Yes."

"Good. Now I know that you are trying to change the subject, but it's not going to work. I'm on it now," I say.

"Change what subject? About that awful accident?"

"Yep. That'd be it. Did I ever tell you the full story?"

"Yes, that you got hit by a drunk driver."

"He wasn't just any drunk driver Sierra." I began to tell her what actually happened. When I turned sixteen, I was on a downward spiral. I missed Sam like crazy and I wanted to be able to celebrate that birthday with him. A friend of mine decided to take me to a house party. I was skeptical but I still went. While I was there, a couple of guys grabbed me, locked me in a room, ripped my clothes off, and tried to rape me but I bit one and dug my fingers into the other one's eye until they let me go. I ran to my car and drove off as fast as I could, trying to get away and I'd almost made it, or so I thought. Trust fund baby, also known as attempted rapist, had followed me and was trying to run me off the road but when that didn't work, he just hit me.

After I tell Sierra the story, she bursts into tears. "Donna, I'm so sorry."

"There's nothing to be sorry about. It's water under the bridge and it wasn't your fault."

"Does anyone else know?"

"No, and I want to keep it that way." What mom did, compared to the trust fund baby, just shows me that I am stronger than most and I will come out on top every time. Sierra starts to cry and through her tears, she manages to say, "Mom did a lot of messed up stuff to you and I don't know why. We were all hurt by Sam's death."

"*We* didn't all cause Sam's death Sierra. We never would have been in that store if I hadn't asked Sam to go with me. Mom had already told me that she was

CHAPTER 5

busy and didn't want to go so she feels like I caused it because we shouldn't have been there and he was trying to save my life. She can't find it in her heart to forgive me for it. He was her only son. I was an accident. For the accident child to be the reason that the son died, the son she prayed so hard to have, it's got to feel like a swift kick to the stomach. So, while I don't agree with it, I guess I am trying to make sense of it. It's the only way I can move past it."

Mom is dying now, so I am faced with the obstacle of either burying the hatchet, and try to enjoy her last few days of life, or being bitter and angry. If I choose the latter, my mom still wins and there is no way that I am letting the Devil's spawn win this round. She has beat me in several battles before, but not this time. Just as I draw this conclusion, Stephen calls. Crap. I forgot to call him back.

"Stephen. How are you? I am so sorry that I didn't call you back. I have been busy planning my sister's wedding."

"Wedding?"

"Yeah. It's a long story and we are both in the car, headed to get some things done for the wedding right now. Can I call you back?'

"Sure Donna."

"Thanks." I know he feels like I just blew him off. I really need to tell him what's going on. I shoot him a quick text that says, "I have a lot going on and my sister wants to make sure my mom can make it to her wedding. It's impromptu. Can I call you in a few hours?" His response is, "Yes." I'm relieved. If being at home has taught me nothing, it's taught me that I need to appreciate the little things.

After running our errands, we finally make it back to my parent's house. It's hard for me to call it "home." Mom asks for me to come and sit with her and I am feeling some kind of way. I walk in her bedroom and Chandler, Sierra, and Nurse Petar all leave. I don't know where dad is. I grab mom's dress and take it to her so that she can see all of the beautiful embellishments.

CHAPTER 5

"Mom, we got your dress while we were out. Do you like it?"

"Yes."

"Do you like the color?"

"Yes."

"Do you like the beading?"

This time she doesn't answer. She just rubs her hand across it several times and then grabs the remote to adjust her bed so she can sit up a little more. I fluff her pillows and put them behind her to help her get more comfortable.

"Donna I didn't just ask for you to come here to apologize about Sam's death. I asked you to come here because I wanted to see you one last t-t-time." She starts coughing uncontrollably and I give her some water. After several gulps, she calms down and continues, "I know that asking you to forgive me will be a stretch, so I won't. But it means a lot to me that you came upon my request."

I sit on the edge of her bed without speaking, wishing I could ask her why she treated me that way but I stubbornly keep it to myself. I didn't come here because she requested it, I came here because my daddy asked me to come and let go of the hurt and I knew, deep down, that I couldn't do that without first facing her. A part of me doesn't want to give her the satisfaction of knowing that she succeeded in breaking me. I will never show her that I am a mess, that I have to be in control. I will never let her know about how much I obsess about the smallest details, just to make sure that I haven't done anything wrong. No. She will have to sit here in wonderment, trying to figure out what is on my mind while I twiddle my thumbs and stare at the wall.

"Donna." Her voice startles me and I jump. "Are you ok? Did I do this to you? You seem so disconnected."

"I'm just hungry." I say as I think to myself. Did she really just ask me if she'd done this to me; as if she doesn't know? I repeat to myself over and over, "I have to be nice. She is dying," until Chandler walks in the room. I can tell that she feels the tension.

"Am I interrupting anything?" She asks.

CHAPTER 5

"No." Mom says but I never look at her. I close my eyes for a moment and then shake it off. I look at Chandler and put on a fake smile, one she can clearly see through.

"I should go," she says.

"Maybe that's best," mom blurts out. Her voice is suddenly strong, and Chandler and I both know she means business. Chandler scurries out the room, closing the door behind her.

"What's your problem Donna?" she asks.

There she is. I have been waiting for this *mom* to show up. I knew she wasn't that innocent mother who wanted to apologize like she pretended to be. I knew it.

"Do you really want to get into it mom?" I ask.

"Yeah. I think I do. You're angry with me, and rightfully so, but you have to let it go."

"No. I don't have to let it go."

What I really want to say to her is that I don't have to let shit go. I don't want to be here with her fake ass, pretending like she is so feeble that she can't construct a sentence without stuttering. I want to tell her that her fake-ass apology means nothing to me and she could have kept it and that the only reason I came back to this house is because my father asked me and he seemed desperate to make her happy. But, I won't give her that much satisfaction to blow up at her. I will just continue to sit and respond dryly because it seems to aggravate her. It's a petty but small win for me.

"Fine Donna. Don't let it go. But you will feel bad when I'm gone and you never spoke your mind."

She may be right. If she dies, I may still have unanswered questions. The difference, though, is that it is my choice to not ask, not hers.

"Mom. Where's dad?" I ask in an effort to change the subject.

"He is outside in the shed. He wants to build a small bridge for the wedding."

"A bridge?"

CHAPTER 5

"Yeah. A bridge to go over the trench in the back yard. He says it will be a nice place to take pictures."

"I need to make sure I order enough flowers for that."

"Don't change the topic at hand Donna. I know you're angry with me. You have every right to be."

"I know."

"So why are you acting like this?"

"Because talking about it won't resolve anything right now. You aren't apologizing to me because you mean it. You are doing it because you want to make your peace before you die. What's wrong? You don't think you can get into heaven unless you make amends for all the stuff you did to me?" I bite my tongue to keep from using expletives towards this woman. I don't want to let her know that she is upsetting me.

"There it is. There's the conversation I have been waiting for Donna."

"Mom. I love you. You birthed me, raised me, and you and dad made sure I had a roof over my head and food in my tummy. For that, I will always love and respect you and for that, I love you. There really is nothing more to talk about."

"You have questions."

"No. I don't."

"Yes. You do. Ask them?"

"I don't have any questions to ask you. If you have something you want to tell me, I am willing to listen."

I stand up and walk towards the window to look at the back yard. I try to imagine what the wedding will look like, think about how the flowers will be arranged and, as I look over the yard, I see the vacant lot behind the house.

"Who does that lot belong to mom?"

"What lot?"

"Behind the house." This is my last-ditch effort to try to change the subject. Hopefully she will take the bait.

"I see we're really doing this Donna," she sighs, "Fine. I won't press you to talk to me anymore. At least, not today. The lot belongs to us."

"It belongs to us?"

"Yeah. I bought it back when you were about sixteen or so." Oh, she bought it with my money. I ask, "Does dad know?"

"Yes. I finally broke down and told him a few years ago because I couldn't pay the taxes on it without his help."

"I see."

"Why?"

"We can get a valet to park the cars back there for the wedding to keep them off the street."

"I see you're full of good ideas."

"I am. It's too bad that you never gave me a chance to show them to you," I snap.

"I deserved that."

"Are you hungry mom?"

"Yes. I am. Are you about to cook?"

"Yeah. I guess I can."

"Will you make me some chicken and dumplings?"

"Sure. I can do that." I'm surprised she asked for that. If someone was mad at me, I wouldn't ask them to make me anything that could potentially hide items that might harm me. The good old "country" in us will pick up a few chicken feet, wash them really good, and throw them in the pot for flavor. Maybe I can put a little hoo-doo on her chicken's foot and make a special pot just for her. I smile to myself at the crazy thought, knowing full well I am not going to try and hurt her, nor do I know anything about hoo-doo. Besides, who am I kidding? She isn't worth that much energy to me to put forth *that* much effort to try to hurt her any more than she has hurt herself. She is dying because guilt is eating away at her, nothing more.

I walk out of the room and head towards the kitchen to get started on the food and check my email at work to make sure everything is under control. I see they are having a Town Hall meeting today at two. I shoot a quick email to Melanie and she tells me that she will send me notes but asks me not to join the call. She also said that she may try to put me on FMLA which will lock me out of the system if things don't improve with my mother. How can imminent death improve? I take

CHAPTER 5

a deep breath before I respond, sitting down at the kitchen table to do so, and let her know that the condition is worsening. I have only been gone for a few days, though, and I tell her that she spoke today and seems to be in better health. I end the email with, "Maybe she will beat this thing. Keep the family in your prayers."

I pick up the phone to call Stephen who answers after about three rings.

"Hey Ms. Lady," he says.

"Hey Stephen."

"It's been hard getting in touch with you since you have been in Georgia. Are you sure you don't have a man out there that I should be worried about?" He says jokingly.

"Well, there is this older gentleman with dimples who has my heart," I respond in jest.

"Nooooooo, I have to compete with a Sugar Daddy!?" he laughs.

"Don't say that. No Sugar Daddies are over here. Besides, my father won't mind me sharing a little bit of my time with you. We'll see."

EIGHT MOMENTS

The conversation goes on for about twenty minutes and I start cooking as we talk playfully. I am getting too comfortable with him. Nope. I am not ready for this. Love hurts like hell when it falls into the wrong hands and the new owner selfishly attempts to break its victim's heart. I am not trying to be its next victim. I imagine love coming to me like a thief in the night, stealing my soul and placing it next to someone who just wants to suck it dry, leaving it completely helpless and left to die away. I don't want any parts of it right now. Let me just be happy for my sister and her new husband-to-be.

"Donna are you ok?" Stephen asks.

"Oh. I'm sorry. I'm fine. I was just thinking about something."

I want to tell him how hard it is to be with me; to try to love someone who is broken. You try to talk to a broken person during difficult times and your words fall on deaf ears. And if they do hear you, they are listening and hear something completely different from what it is you are trying to say. No matter how hard you try, your love can't save them and there is nothing you can do to open their heart. That's me right now. I'm trying to figure it all out.

"It's your mom, isn't it?" He asks.

"Yeah. That's it." I lie.

"I can only imagine what it is like to know you are about to lose a parent Donna." He pauses as if he is trying to find something else to say. He can sense something isn't right so he ends with, "I know you're cooking dinner for your mom. Go ahead and finish. You can call me back. Ok?"

"Sure. That sounds good," I say. It *sounds* good. Maybe Stephen will be a good distraction for me; a rescue from all of the drama of which I keep finding myself in the middle. Or am I kidding myself?

"Actually," I say, "I'm not ready to get off the phone just yet. Can you talk a little longer?"

"I'm glad you don't and I can talk for as long as you'd like."

"Good. But I have a question."

EIGHT MOMENTS

"Shoot."

"What happened between you and your daughter's mom? I may be out of line but I'm curious." I need to find out what I am dealing with now before any more time is wasted between us.

"She's my ex-wife."

"Ok. What happened between you and your ex-wife, if you don't mind my asking?"

"I don't mind at all. The short story of it all is that we wanted two different things in life. She doesn't want to work, but wants the finer things in life, she blows through money like its water, and, when she didn't get her way, she cheated on me with a guy I'd always thought was her "best friend.""

"What did you do?" My question throws him off guard.

"What do you mean?"

"When we were at the grocery store, she seemed angry, like she hated your guts and when you speak of the restrictions she places on you in terms of your daughter, it reminds me of the wrath of a scorned and bitter woman. So, what did you do?"

There was a long pause and then he laughs a bit.

"You're quite intuitive, aren't you? I didn't do anything while we were married. I'm not that guy. After the divorce, though, I made sure she knew she was missing out on a good thing. I'd been working on a deal to start my business that I knew would be able to afford the lifestyle she wanted to live. All I asked for was a little patience. So, when she handed me the divorce papers, and moved out, I halted the deal and waited until the divorce was over. It allowed me the opportunity to renegotiate some terms which proved very lucrative. She feels like she deserves half of it, and she tried to take me to court for it, but the judge wouldn't give it to her. She has hated me ever since."

"So, she hates you because of the money?" I ask, feeling like something is missing in this story.

"Well…that and the fact that I was being petty and slept with one of her good friends just to get back at her."

"Yeah. That was petty."

"I know and I am paying for it now. I shouldn't have done it because I didn't care enough to hurt her. I was just upset that she tried to take everything I'd worked for so that we could have a better life and didn't value the love in the relationship more than a nice house to brag on, a few designer bags, and expensive shoes. I never wanted my daughter to be in a broken home and she knew that, even tried to use it to get me to come back to her after the divorce."

"Did you try to make it work?"

"I tried, but it wasn't the same and I knew she was only after the money. She didn't really love me."

"Hunh..." I inadvertently say while deep in thought.

"Does that answer all of your questions?" he asks.

"For now."

"Well, what about you? Why aren't you in a relationship?"

"I got played and cheated on in my last serious relationship and then I got active in the community. Relationships for

CHAPTER 5

me just kind of…fell by the wayside and I have been celibate for about five years."

"Interesting."

"Not really. Not interesting at all. Listen, my father just walked in, can I call you back?"

"Sure you can."

"Great. Thanks. I'll call you later this evening." As I'm hanging up, I'm sure he heard me ask my daddy to taste the dumplings and I did that intentionally. I don't want him to think I am avoiding his last question.

-6-

Lost and Found

I'm having trouble sleeping in this house and I just can't get comfortable. There are too many demons haunting me. Shadows of the night look like people from my past and my ears somehow hear whispered words which remind me of conversations once held with my brother. Staples around the house represent a lot of pain. There's the grandfather clock I accidentally broke when I was trying to wind it and my grandmother's favorite chair that I had to sit in as punishment when I'd done something of which my mom didn't approve. I want to go back to Houston and escape all of this, but I can't. I figure planning a special night on the town for Sierra will help her get her mind off of mom's rapidly declining health. At some point, we all will have to face the fact that she is not going to be here much

CHAPTER 6

longer. Both of my sisters are reluctant to leave, but I really think mom and dad need some alone time. They have shared a love for almost forty years, that is no easy feat. For his sake, I hope her death doesn't keep him from living. There can be no mistake that he loves her wholeheartedly. He stands up for her, even in her wrongs and, together, they have always shown a united front to outsiders. Sure, they have had their arguments like any other couple, especially over me, but they love each other all the same. I used to wonder how my dad could overlook some of the things she would do to me and how he could love her so much. It seemed that he tried to make it up to me in his own little special way. But, as I got older, I realized that it worked for them. I have seen a lot of relationships come and go. People get lazy and want to walk away because they can't get their way or are too selfish to see what they are doing wrong. My parents, however, seem to have a different perspective so I just stopped wondering and, instead, started longing for someone to love me the way he loves her.

EIGHT MOMENTS

Like the few nights before, I get up, slide on my night gown, put on my slippers, and head for the kitchen. This time, though, I decided I didn't want water and went straight for the good stuff. My parents had no idea that we knew where the stash was, and that was a good thing. I'd really like to finish the conversation I was having with Stephen the other day, but I've been so busy planning the wedding with my sister that I have only been able to share a little bit of small talk with him. It has been nice getting to know him. I grab a snifter out of the bar cabinet and the short bottle of D'ussé XO and pour myself a drink, neat. There are just some days that I don't want, or need, ice. I take a sip, savoring the notes of blackberry, chocolate, and some kind of nut and I'm taken aback by how smooth it is. I examine the bottle that bears the *Cross of Lorraine*. Very plain and simple, yet powerful. I continue to savor the flavor of the cognac as I settle down comfortably on the couch. Do I turn on the TV? Do I sit here in silence? I really don't want to wake my family, so I guess I will just chill out. I reflect on the last conversation I had with mom. I knew she was faking that nice guy routine. Maybe in her sick, twisted way my mom wants me here for my dad and sisters because she definitely didn't plan to be nice to me. In her defense, one compliment she has always given me is that I am the strongest of the siblings. Hell, when you've gone through what I have gone through, you have to be strong. Whether I like it or not, I have to thank her for making me this way. I have learned a lot from the people closest to me. My mom made me learn how to be strong, to be a fighter. My father showed me unconditional love and compassion, sometimes to a fault. My brother Sam, by saving me, taught me courage. Sierra's unwavering optimism won't let me be negative, even when I want to be and especially not around her and Chandler taught me structure and the importance of loving myself. Since we have all been preoccupied with making sure mom comfortable and planning Sierra's wedding, I haven't had a chance to have a heart-to-heart with Chandler and I really need one right now. She is the one who saw my mom's cruelty towards me, and actually confronted her about it. It got her slapped in the mouth, but she still did it. Even afterwards, she questioned daddy about it, asking why mom was being mean to me. Chandler *is* the chatty one. I admire her honesty and truthfulness.

After about an hour, and finishing the bottle of D'ussé, I stumble to bed. I haven't had that much to drink in one sitting in years and I need to get some rest because we have a long day tomorrow. I need to call all of the vendors to make sure they will all be on time, check on the liquor delivery for the open bar, and make sure that all of the ladies Chandler invited to our surprise dinner party for Sierra will be ready when the limo arrives to pick them up. I write a quick message to Chandler, and schedule it to send at 8:00 A.M. I don't want to wake her up right now. I want to try to make this day as special as possible for Sierra because I know she is worried. I grab my glass and take it to the sink, grab a BC powder and a Vitamin-C pack and take them both so that I can

CHAPTER 6

function tomorrow without a headache or hangover. Once in bed, I spend about thirty precious minutes lying there with my eyes closed before I finally drift off to sleep.

The sun starts to peek through the windows, and the birds are chirping. I hear a little woodpecker outside on the tree, and people are hustling about in the house. I decide to see what is going on and walk over to the door. There are too many unfamiliar voices and a lot of strange noises so I decide to crack open the door but can't see much so I walk out into the hallway to find out what's going on. I see a couple of men hovered over my mom. I blink a couple of times to make sure my eyes aren't playing tricks on me. This can't be happening. I grab a pair of pants and a bra out of my suitcase and hurriedly put them on to find out what is happening. I stand beside mom and ask her if she is ok but it is my dad's voice that answers, "No. She is not ok." She shoots him a dirty look and waves him off with a flick of her hand. "I'm fine Donna, just a little dehydrated. These guys are just making me comfortable." Strangely, a look of worry glides across her face. It's a look I have never seen before and I am stunned.

"What do you need me to do?" I ask.

"Nothing Ma'am," one of the guys answers.

"So...you're from hospice?"

"Yes. Your mom will be fine."

He says she will be fine but he, too, has a strange look on his face. I walk over to dad and stand beside him. He puts his arm around my shoulder and pulls me close to him. My dad is vulnerable.

"Dad. Is there something you want to talk to me about?" I ask him, hoping he will open up, but he looks surprised. He has been sliding down a slippery slope since he found out my mom is fighting for her life and she isn't making it any better. She has been milking this sympathy as much as she can. "Why do you think I need to talk to you about something? Did your..." he starts to say but my mom interrupts him and says, "Sh-sh-she's just worried about you. You can see it in her f-f-face." She takes a deep

CHAPTER 6

breath and her lips start turning a little bluish. You can't fake that. Something is really wrong. "Are you cold mom?" I ask her. She shakes her head up and down, and I grab a blanket. The men won't let me cover her up just yet so I grab a couple of her thinner blankets and head towards the dryer. Maybe if I heat them up, that will help and they will be nice and warm for her to cuddle under.

"She will be in a tent in the back yard tomorrow for my sister's wedding," I say to one of the gentleman, "is that going to be ok?" He frowns but says, "She should be fine, just make sure that she doesn't leave the house." He turns his back to me and I walk out the door. I don't know what to do. My father is visibly upset and he won't talk to me to help make it better. I am not used to seeing him this way and it is making me rethink leaving him alone with mom tonight while we take Sierra out. "Dad. I will stay here with you and mom and let Chandler handle things with Sierra. It will give me time to prepare for tomorrow anyway," I say to him from the hallway. I turn around to see him smiling at me, shaking his head from side-to-side. "No Bay-girl," he says, "Your mother and I haven't had any true alone time in a while. This will be good for us. You go out and have fun with your sisters. I think you need it." He walks over and kisses me on the forehead then turns around to go back to the room. After about ten minutes, I grab the blankets out of the dryer and wrap them around my mother. I stand in the corner, not knowing what to say to her, so I tell her, "Mom. No matter what has happened between us, I love you." She doesn't hear me though, she's already fallen asleep.

I check my work email to see if I got something from Melanie. Tom can handle the rest. Sure enough, it was an important message to the team. It reads:

Team,
We've all been focusing on improving the customer experience while watching the bottom line. Unfortunately, it has not been enough and we are about to experience some forced job loss. I will be

CHAPTER 6

speaking to each of you with more details as soon as possible.

I knew this mess was coming. I shoot Melanie a quick email to ask her how she wants me to handle this situation since I am, technically, out on vacation. I have a bad feeling about this.

Well now that I know my job is on the line, I can prepare for what's next. Or can I? I pick up the phone and send messages to Maggie and JoAnn, respectively. Each message tells them about the email I received from Melanie and that my job is in jeopardy. Even if my mom is on her deathbed, that woman doesn't like me and, if she has her choice, I am going to be the first to go. JoAnn responds with all the positivity in the world, telling me that I am an asset and they will be sorry if they lose me. But, if I am let go from the company, she has an opening at her non-profit organization that just opened and she will leave the position open for me. Maggie's response was similar, telling me that she knows of a few positions that I need to go ahead and apply for before the end of the day. I'm skeptical of making any moves right now, especially with the uncertainty of my mother's health, but I know that I have to make a move soon. I ask Maggie for the job requisition numbers and tell JoAnn that I will let her know. I'd love to work with JoAnn, but I already volunteer quite a bit there and the pay cut will be considerable. I decide not to think about it anymore. I need to go back to bed to get some rest but I know that I can't. It's time to make those phone calls to the vendors.

After confirming that everything will be delivered on time, we are ready for this sunset wedding. It's going to be beautiful. We have managed to pull off an entire wedding in a matter of days, thanks to Sierra's anticipation of her upcoming nuptials and her storage full of items she's been purchasing over the last few months. In my down time, I have to call Stephen. I have really been blowing him off. Maybe my first thought was right. I don't need to involve him in my mess-of-a-life right now. I dial his number, but he doesn't answer so I leave a message for him to give me a call

CHAPTER 6

and before I can end the message, he calls me back.

"Hey you," I answer.

"Hey lady." He responds.

"It's been a crazy week."

"I can tell."

"Are you ok?"

"Yes. I am. I've been wondering the same about you."

"My mom had a bad morning and my job is about to let some people go, so it's been...interesting, to say the least."

"That's not quite the word I would use, but ok. We can go with that." He chuckles and I am glad. At least he isn't upset with me; for now. My thoughts about him are all over the place. One minute I want to get to know him, the next minute I don't want to involve him in my chaos. I really need to figure out what I want to do.

"When did you say you will be in Atlanta?" I ask. Insert foot-in-mouth right here. I don't know what I want to do but I am asking him about his plans.

"Next week. I will be there for two weeks."

EIGHT MOMENTS

"Ok. I think I will be here also. My mom's health is declining fast," I say this to him against my better judgment. I don't need to make plans to meet with this man any time soon. But, I feel drawn to him and intrigued.

I know this is mean of me to say, but I am really surprised that my mother is sick. I always thought evil people lived longer so that they can torment the good people in their lives.

"Stephen. I don't want you to think that I blew you off the other day." Here I go again with my big mouth, thinking one thing and saying another.

"No. I get it. You are at home with your family for a very serious reason. I don't expect to take up your entire day. I'm just glad you let me in on a few snippets of it. It's also nice that you are excited about seeing me when I come in town." Why does he have to be so understanding?

"Excited? I don't believe I used the word 'excited', did I?" I ask.

"Not directly, but I can feel it in my bones. It comes from the words you

CHAPTER 6

say. I'm good at reading between the lines."

"Mmmmhmmm, is that what you got out of what I said? If so, I need to re-evaluate my words in future conversations."

"See. Right there. You are predicting future conversations."

"But, I didn't say…"

"Shhhh…" he playfully laughs, "Just let it flow. You know I'm worth getting to know."

"A big ego to go with that big smile, I see?" I say, laughing along.

We play back and forth until my father calls my name.

"Listen, my father is calling me Stephen. I have a lot to do. I will call you back if it's not too late."

"It's never too late to call me. But, do whatever you feel is comfortable for you.

"I will try to call you soon. But we have a busy day ahead of us for the next couple of days."

"That's fine. Have a good day Ms. Lady."

EIGHT MOMENTS

After hanging up, I begin to think that maybe I really should give him a chance. He has pretty good conversation, and a sense of humor and I like that. I will figure it out soon. Right now, I have other things to worry about.

I walk down the hallway to see what my father needs. My mom is vomiting and that isn't good, especially since they just stabilized her from dehydration earlier this morning. I run to my parent's bathroom and grab a towel and run it under cold water then give it to my father before going back to the kitchen to get some ice for her to suck on. Dad had gotten a bag of ice so mom can have small pieces to put in her mouth, so I grab some of the smallest pieces I can find and take it to him. When I walk in the room, I see that he is now gently rubbing her back and I watch him until he notices me. Her eyes are closed, so she seems relaxed. I study his face. His smooth sun-kissed skin and gray hair both complement each other very well but I am beginning to see worry lines form by his eyes. He finally looks up at the doorway which startles me a bit.

CHAPTER 6

"Hand me the glass baby. Your mother needs it," he says as he reaches towards me. His words are dripping with worry and concern and it makes my heart skip a beat. I hand him the glass as I try to imagine how he feels. Is he going to be ok after mom is gone? He will be in this house all alone and with Sierra newly married and Chandler with her own family, no one will be in the house to keep him busy. Let's be honest, there is no way in hell I am moving back here. No sir. No way. Maybe I shouldn't say that. Every time I say that I will never do something, life has a way of telling me it has other plans. I leave the bedroom and walk back to my room.

I finally decide to unpack my bags. It looks like I will be here for longer than I thought, and I can't keep living out of my suitcase. I just hate to get too comfortable because I always leave something behind when I do. I walk over to the chest of drawers and open the top drawer. To my surprise, there were clothes in there that belonged to me before I left. I begin to sift through them and notice one of my favorite t-shirts. I pick it up and smell it and my senses are flooded as thoughts of my childhood come rushing in like a raging river. Tears come to my eyes as I rub the shirt against my face. Sam gave me this shirt and I thought I'd lost it. I slide down to the floor, holding the shirt close to me, crying so heavily that I belt out in agony. I never thought I would experience this type of pain again. But, in this moment, I feel a grief that is inexplicable and a sharpness in my chest as my heart begins to beat faster than normal. My body grows hot, and I start to sweat. I feel nauseous and my limbs start to feel heavy but I refuse to let the t-shirt go. I'd looked everywhere for this shirt, even called back and asked my mom about it and she told me no one had seen it, making the snide remark, "Maybe you would have it if you hadn't high-tailed your ass out of here so fast the day you left." She knew that shirt meant a lot to me. So why not tell me that she'd found it?

I lose control of all of my functions and finally crumble into a pile on the floor and my head thumps as it hits the ground,

CHAPTER 6

no longer able to hold myself up. I continue to cry heavily, until I black-out, my t-shirt has fallen on my chest.

I wake up to Chandler and Sierra standing over me.

"Are you ok?" Chandler asks. She and Sierra try to help me stand up as Chandler calls out to dad.

"No," I say to her, "Don't call dad. It will just be one more thing for him to worry about." But, I was too late and he was already entering the room, ducking his head so that it won't hit the top of the door frame. She helps me walk over to the bed so that I can wake up. I think I passed out. Somehow, I am still clinging onto my t-shirt. I take a deep breath and fold it gently. I'm not going to ask mom why she didn't tell me she knew where the shirt was. It's not even worth the aggravation today. This is Sierra's day and I plan on making it special for her before she gets married.

"Are you alright Bay-girl? What happened?" Dad asked.

"I think she passed out daddy," Chandler says.

EIGHT MOMENTS

Daddy walks over to me and touches my forehead. He leans in a little closer and smiles. It's his first sincere smile I have seen since he first picked me up. I smile back and tell him, "I'm alright daddy. I'll be fine." I start to stand up slowly, until I catch my balance, and walk over to my suitcase where I safely place my t-shirt. I turn to look at all of them staring at me. They are speechless, partly because they all know how much that shirt means to me, and they knew I had been asking about it for years. Chandler finally comes out and says, "Uhhh Donna, where did you find your shirt?"

"Did you know where it was?" I ask.

"No. I looked everywhere for it and I think I speak for all of us when I say that we are shocked you have it."

"It was in the bedroom chest."

"The bedroom chest?"

"Yep. I found it in the top drawer."

"I looked in there several times Donna. That can't be possible."

CHAPTER 6

My dad shakes his head from side-to-side in disbelief which leads me to believe that we share similar thoughts, that my mom had something to do with the shirt's disappearance. Something, however, is really odd. Sierra does not seem herself and she doesn't utter a word. I look at her and ask what's wrong to which she replies, "Nothing." Not willing to allow her to brush me off so easily, I ask again, "Sierra, what's wrong?" Instead of answering, she walks over and hugs me then whispers in my ear that mom told her to put the t-shirt in the drawer right before I got home. "I didn't know it was going to affect you like this. I'm sorry," she says. I want to break away from her hold but I know she didn't mean any harm so I just hug her tighter, telling her that it will be ok. Still, I wonder how she didn't know that it would affect me this way. Like Chandler said, everyone in the house was looking for it. More importantly, everyone knew that it was my favorite shirt, that it was the last thing Sam gave me, and that I was devastated when I couldn't find it.

EIGHT MOMENTS

"I'm fine," I say to her and decide to change the subject. I pull away and ask, "What time will you be ready tonight?"

"You still want to go?"

"Of course. You know I do."

My dad smiles sincere smile number two, and says, "I guess you guys don't need me. He shoots a look of desperation to Chandler, thinking I didn't notice it, and ducks his head again as he walks out the door. It seems like my room is the only room that has the shorter door frame. He doesn't have to do it anywhere else in the house. A feeling of anger rushes over me when I think about my mother putting Sierra in the middle of her mess, but I take a deep breath and try to think positively. Maybe mom has an explanation and she thought that she was doing something nice for me by returning it, knowing I'd find it in the drawer. Yeah. That's the narrative I will go with. I like that thought much better.

Sierra walks out the room to go to the bathroom and a part of me wants to question Chandler about the look between her and dad but I decide to side on the err

CHAPTER 6

of caution and not ask about it so that I can get through this day. I look at Chandler, staring a hole in her head and flailing my arms until I get her attention. When she finally notices me, I mouth the words, "What time will the limo be here?" She raises her hands and shows seven fingers just as Sierra walks back into the room.

"Sierra, don't forget that you and I are going out to eat with Chandler at seven," I say. I can't wait to see her face when she realizes that all of her friends are waiting inside a limo. She has no idea what we are doing for her and thinks Chandler is driving.

"I brought my clothes with me, I just need to freshen my make-up and put on my clothes and I will be ready," she says.

"Wait. What time is it?" I ask, not knowing how long I was passed out.

"It's only 3:30."

"Oh. Ok. I look out the window and see the sunlight outside. I was about to panic.

"Wait. The people are supposed to be here to set up the tent for the wedding. They should have arrived at three o'clock."

"They did," Sierra said, "That's how we found you on the floor. When the people came, we were calling your name and you never answered. They are in the back yard now."

"Ok. Let me put some clothes on so we can go check on it and make sure they brought everything we ordered." I go in my suitcase and grab my toiletries, underwear, leggings, and my infamous *Unapologetically Me* t-shirt, then head off to the bathroom to freshen up before I go outside. I think I'll hold off on unpacking for now. I don't need, or want any more surprises.

After a quick shower, and fixing my hair, I hurriedly finish cleaning myself up so that I can run outside. Ms. Sherry is delivering the flower wall today at five so I at least need to have that area set up and ready to go. Finally dressed, I walk towards the living room so I can head outside. It is beautiful. My big sister will have the wedding of her dreams and I can't be any more excited for her. I walk over to the team and introduce myself, asking for the person in charge when I see a young man, who appears to be in his twenties, standing in the corner with a clipboard. He seems to be focused on getting the job completed. When he sees me approach him, he places the clipboard behind his back in an effort to greet me properly.

"You must be Donna? I'm Ramón." He says.

"Guilty," I say with a smile as I hold out my hand to shake his.

"It's a pleasure to meet you. We are almost done. Your back yard was easier than I thought. How do you like the lighted dance floor?"

"I love it. My sister is going to remember this special night. Did you bring the pipe and drapes also?"

"Yes. The design team is working on putting everything together. Your flower wall can go over there, in the corner. I know you wanted the option of placing it outside but the meteorologists are predicting rain and I don't want to ruin anything." He points to the far-right corner in the front behind the wedding party table and I look over to examine the space. It looks big enough for the wall.

"Ok. Great. Ms. Sherry will be here to deliver it at five." I say.

"Well everything is almost in place so she will be good to go when she arrives."

I thank Ramón, and slowly examine the room. It looks like everything is in place and they put the tables and chairs where I'd planned. This is going to be amazing.

Sierra walks to the tent and is very pleased. She starts to put out some of the decorations she purchased after finding out that we can lock the tent tonight. She pulls out boxes she'd previously stored in the shed and creates a table at the front entrance with pictures of her and Aaron. To my surprise, she has a large engagement picture and an easel. She tells me that there is another one of her in her dress but we can't reveal it until the wedding starts and everyone is seated. She leaves it in the shed and asks me to move it after the

CHAPTER 6

wedding is over and put it in place before the reception begins. Ms. Sherry arrived a little early and asked Chandler if she can see mom but was refused. She walks out to the back with us and tells us of her encounter. "She has been sleeping a lot lately and has a few bad episodes Ms. Sherry," I say, "You will see her tomorrow though. She frowns at me, but accepts my response and begins to build the flower wall in the designated area.

"To tell you the truth," she says, "I'm glad you decided to get a tent. It's nicer. These air conditioning units are working well too. It's cold in here." She continues to build the wall and place the vases on the tables. Your wall will be fine tomorrow. The buds will have opened enough for gorgeous pictures. I will bring the rest of the flowers tomorrow morning. I want them to be fresh and don't want them to droop." She hugs me and says, "You've done a great job here. It's beautiful and it's also good to see you." She touches my cheek and then walks away, her words, "See you in the morning," trail behind her.

EIGHT MOMENTS

Sierra and I continue to put decorations in place until almost six-thirty, so we have to hurry and get dressed. I receive a text from Chandler saying they will be at the house at seven o'clock sharp and we need to be ready because we have reservations for eight o'clock in Braselton at *Local Station*. She also says she made hangover bags. Thank goodness. I want to stick to old faithful, though, and I think Sierra should too so after we are dressed, I hand her a bottle of water and tell her to take a BC powder and a Vitamin-C packet. Chandler doesn't know it yet, but she is going to do the same when I get in the limo. All three of us are in the wedding tomorrow so we can't afford to be hungover.

The surprise on Sierra's face is priceless when she realizes we got her a limo and all of her friends are gathered inside. She literally starts crying and hugging everyone. It's a special moment. I'd hired a photographer to ride along with us and take some candid shots and she is lost so we have to wait a few minutes for her to arrive. Chandler had stocked the

CHAPTER 6

bar in the limo, so we are ready for a good time. I place the "I'm the bride" sash on Sierra that I'd picked up for her and we head out for a hell of a night. It seems like Chandler may have already hit the bottle because she is a little giggly. I slide close to her and grab a bottle of water. "Here. Take this." She gulps down the water and the BC powder without arguing with me then tells me not to let her drink anything else until we have eaten.

We arrive at the restaurant at 7:55, just in time for our eight o'clock reservations. We decided to get two of each of some of the sides. Our friendly server, Jeanette, has a bubbly personality and is taking really good care of us. She suggests that we try the New Orleans Shrimp and Grits and the fourteen-ounce ribeye steak but I have my eye on the Chicken Caprese. Chandler orders the shrimp linguine and Sierra orders the stuffed pork chop. The other four girls Shai, Krys, Dru, and the photographer, Kensington all order the Artichoke Chicken, the Black Angus Ribeye, Surf N' Turf, and the Manhattan Strip, respectively. When the food arrives at our table, it is a magnificent feast. Our table has a full display of sautéed baby spinach, wild mushroom risotto, glazed baby carrots, and sweet potato fries along with all of the entrees that we ordered. The steaks were sizzling and look extremely succulent and the baby carrots are my favorite of the side dishes. They are plated like they belong in a food magazine. The glaze is a perfect blend of sweet and salty, with flavors that pop in your mouth, one after another. When I cut into them, they are just the right amount of tenderness, yet firm enough to not be considered mushy. I spoon a few more onto my plate and dig into my Chicken Caprese. The tomatoes are bursting in my mouth, juicy and succulent. The mozzarella cheese is melted perfectly and the hint of balsamic vinegar gives it a pop. The chicken is juicy and tender. Mixed with the herb couscous and spinach, my meal is a hit. We sit at the table and laugh with Sierra's friends as we each sip from the drinks we ordered from the bar.

CHAPTER 6

Dru shares the story of how Aaron and Sierra met at the nursing home and how excited Sierra was when she called her to talk about him. Sierra blushes as she looks down at her pear-shaped diamond ring, two carats to be exact. It's beautiful yet simple, but it is Sierra's style. Krys and Shai tell us about a vacation they all went on. Sierra almost killed herself trying to answer a call from Aaron because he'd been out of the country on business. They were in the mountains and Sierra took off running to grab her phone but fell midway and slid the rest.

"She almost broke her neck!" Krys says. We continue to share stories, but I feel a little out of place. Sure, I have stories of my own, but I don't have the connection with Sierra's friends that Chandler has because I don't know them. I glance at Kensington, who is busy taking pictures between bites and then Chandler, who can feel that I am uncomfortable so she says, "I brought gift bags ladies *and* let's open Sierra's presents." She has quickly changed the mood and I am thankful.

EIGHT MOMENTS

Sierra is beaming with gratitude as she opens her presents. Her friends have given her gift cards and lingerie for her wedding night. Chandler and I pooled our money together to get Sierra a massage tomorrow before the wedding. We want her to be relaxed. The massage therapist will be at the house at three. She has an hour session, and her make-up artist is arriving at 4:30. Sierra starts to cry again and reaches over to hug me and Chandler. "Thank you for making this day so special guys," she says tearfully.

"Don't cry. You will have all of us over here in tears," I say.

Chandler tells everyone to open their bags and take their hangover medicine now. As she and I motion to Jeanette to bring us the check. The two of us split it and give Jeanette a hefty tip and then we all pack back into the limo. Chandler has a surprise for us, told us to drink up, and the ride begins.

Shai looks at me quizzically before asking, "You live in Houston, right?"

"Right," I say.

CHAPTER 6

"Do you like it there?" she asks. Her words are starting to drag so I can tell she is starting to feel the liquor buzz. Slurred words are never a good thing.

"It's ok."

"It has to be more than ok because you never come home."

"You're right." Here we go. I should have known that this was coming. I look at my sisters, who are both buzzing by the way, and know they can't get me out of this conversation. In fact, Chandler is so oblivious, she turns the music up and starts dancing with Sierra and Dru. I take a deep breath and ask her, "What is it that you really want to ask me Shai?"

"Nothing. I just wonder why you never come home," she yells just as Chandler accidentally turned the radio off while trying to turn the volume up some more. Any buzz I may have had is now gone. I don't want to talk about why I don't come home. It's none of Shai's business. Chandler can see I'm getting irritated and says, "Why are you worried about Donna and how often she comes home? We are here to celebrate Sierra and enjoy her last night as a single woman."

"You're right," Shai says.

"I know," says Chandler. You've got to love my sis Chan. She will get you told quickly, and dare you to say something back. As the night continues, I realize I need to hold back on the drinking because these heifers are crazy. They are knocking them back like water. Meanwhile, I'm sipping and watching the drama unfold, as is Kensington who is getting some great shots. By the time we make it to the "surprise" Chandler has, no one is in shape to go inside. I'm tired, Sierra's asleep, and Shai, Dru, and Krys are drunk out of their minds. I let the window down to talk to the driver and ask him to take us to the nearest CVS or Walgreens but Sierra awakens and is ready to party some more. I dig through my purse to find some more B.C. powders and hand them to the ladies. Chandler pulls me to the side and says, "It's 11:30. We need to be out of here in an hour." I don't want to be in here anyway. I think strip clubs are so cliché

CHAPTER 6

for bachelorettes so I start counting down immediately.

We go inside and the first thing Krys wants to do is order some chicken wings. Now I have had my share of some good strip club chicken wings, but we just ate, and this chick had the fourteen-ounce angus. Why is she hungry? I look at her and roll my eyes but I realize that the greasy food may be what they all need. "Let's find a seat and then grab a waitress," I say but Chandler informs us that she already reserved a section and the hostess takes us to our seats, right in front of the main stage. I do not want booty-juice all over my food but I roll with it because I am not that hungry anyway. I grab the waitress's attention and we place our order for chicken wings and a few drinks.

By the time the food arrives, we have already been there for almost forty minutes. There goes the theory that we are leaving in an hour. At 12:30 I get Chandler's attention to tell her that it's time to go and she helps me gather all the women. Sierra looks pooped and she is ready to leave as well so I am thankful.

EIGHT MOMENTS

As we all pile back into the limo, everyone talks about how much fun they have had tonight. They are still all buzzing from the liquor so they start talking about the strip club and the pimp that was walking around, fully dressed in his loud green suit and cane. Chandler looks at me and says, "Speaking of pimps. Donna, remember when momma told you that you needed to get a sugar daddy to take care of you? You were pissed." Of course I was pissed, I was seventeen and mom had just stolen all of my money. "I don't want to talk about that right now Chan," I say.

"I just want you to know…" she slides over to me and begins to loudly whisper, "I just want you to know that mom was wrong for that. I have seen some of the stuff she has done to you when she didn't think I was paying attention."

"Me too," Sierra yells.

"I don't want to talk about this right now you two. It's not the place." I look over at the girls and all of them are asleep except for Kensington, who is preoccupied with taking shots of the

CHAPTER 6

sleeping beauties, and Shai, who has a smirk on her face. It's like she knows something about me that she wants me to know.

"What's funny Shai?" I ask.

"Nothing much. I just knew there was a reason why you never come home. Now it all makes sense," she says.

"Chandler told you to mind your business because she was being polite. I'm not Chandler and this is not what you want," I say, looking at her sternly. She seems to get the picture. Once again, Sierra sits quietly, like she is hiding something which means she must have mentioned something to Shai about my relationship with my mom. I look at Chandler, disappointed that she let the drinks take over her mouth to air out family business in front of strangers and we ride the rest of the way home in silence.

After dropping off the girls at their homes, we finally make it to our parent's house. Kensington tells us that she got some beautiful sister moments, and other great shots and she can't wait to deliver them to us. She asks me to give her about three weeks. I pay her for her services and Chandler pays for the limo and we all head inside.

"Get some rest Ms. Catchings. Tomorrow you will be Mrs. Duprés," I say to Sierra before checking in on daddy. She pulls me and Chandler into a tight group hug, and then kisses each of us on the cheek. "Thank you for a great night guys," she says. Chandler knows I am a little upset with her for bringing up the Sugar Daddy thing so she just hugs me again and tells me good night before heading into her old room. I peep in my parent's room to see them both sleeping. Daddy is under a blanket in the La-Z-boy chair, with his feet propped up and mom is resting peacefully in the bed. I gently close the door and walk to my room. As crazy as it was, it was a great night.

-7-

Removed
&
Replaced

Sierra's wedding day is finally here and we are still feeling like so much needs to be done. It's seven in the morning and vendors have already begun showing up to set up. Ms. Sherry's flower arrangements are gorgeous, made up of yellow roses and yellow peonies with a touch of baby's breath and she gave us some small floral arrangements made of baby's breath to put down the aisle we created between the tables in the tent. They will be perfect to offset the small lanterns Sierra bought to place down the aisle and are a great compliment to the flower wall. "Who is going to help momma get dressed?" Sierra asks me as we hustle about the house.

"Chandler is," I say. I continue to check off all of the vendors on my list to make sure everyone is here.

"Where is the cake?" Sierra asks.

"They will be here in an hour and the photographer should be here any minute so go to your suite," I say, referring to the living room. Chandler and I put everything we will need to get dressed in the living room and turned it into her wedding suite for the day. We even decorated it so that she can feel comfortable. It is big enough for us to all move around while getting dressed, and can be closed off from everyone else. Aaron will arrive already dressed. He spent the evening with his friends at the hotel where they reserved their honeymoon suite. One of the photographers is meeting him there to capture him as he gets dressed and will ride over in the limo.

"Where are the caterers?"

"Go to your suite and put some clothes on for the pictures. Have you even

CHAPTER 7

bathed this morning or checked on mom and dad?"

"No. I'll go do that now. I'm just so nervous."

"Everything will be fine. What's important is the marriage, not the wedding and mom will be there. This wedding is going to be perfect Sierra. I'll make sure of it."

I look back down at my list of vendors. It looks like everyone is here. The next round of vendors won't come until three this afternoon. I go to the back yard and make sure everyone has what they need. With all of the people moving about the tent, it still feels very cool inside. That's perfect. Aaron's friend brought the sound system over last night while we were out so the DJ and band can connect to it, and the white drapes in the tent are beautiful. They installed lighting that will automatically turn on at six and will alternate between aqua blue, green, and yellow throughout the night and the chandeliers hanging from the ceiling are sparkling from the lighting. It's beautiful. To look at it, you'd think that we'd been planning this wedding for months. I pull out a box of the champagne bottles I got for the party favors and start lining them on the table by the door but I need some help so I walk the short distance to the back door and call out to Chandler.

"Chandler can you come here for a minute?" I say.

"What do you need?" she asks, walking towards me.

"Can you look at this table and make sure that it works as the party favor table?"

"You did a good job. When did you have time to make all of the decorations on the table? You even got a birdcage for the envelopes!"

"Oh, I started on them as soon as I got a chance after Sierra took me to the arts & crafts store."

"The table is beautiful Donna. I should've hired you to plan my wedding." She laughs.

"You know mom wouldn't have allowed that."

"Yeah. I know."

"Your wedding was beautiful too."

CHAPTER 7

"Yeah. Mom did a great job. Maybe you got that skill from her?"

"Let's see. Stubbornness? Check. Ability to be strong? Check. Creativity? Not so much."

"Donna! Mom is creative."

"Creative with spending money to have someone else do it." We both laugh and Chandler becomes serious.

"Sooo...I want to talk to you about last night. Good call on the BC powder and Vitamin-C packet by the way. I don't even feel like I had a drink."

"What about last night? And you're welcome," I say.

"I want to apologize. I was out of line and I don't want to blame it on the alcohol."

"It's no big deal."

"Yes, it is."

"No. It's really not. What do you expect from a woman who stole from me and took me off the insurance policy daddy had for us?"

"Took you off the insurance policy?"

EIGHT MOMENTS

"Yes ma'am. You didn't know? We found out when you went to college that first year, before you came back home. Sierra knows about it. I'm kind of shocked that she didn't tell you." I mumble under my breath, "She tells you everything else."

"What happened Donna?"

"This is not the time, or place, to talk about this. We have to get everything ready for Sierra's wedding," I say.

"Everything is practically done and you need to get inside anyway to be in some of the pictures. Talk to me about it now, or later. You decide!" Chandler says, placing her hand on her hip and cocks her head to the left side.

"Later," I say. Truthfully, I have no intention of talking about it ever. Chandler gives me a strange look and walks off, signaling to me that this isn't over, no matter what I think. Shit. This is going to be an issue. I give the tent a once-over, then follow behind her but detour to my parent's room.

CHAPTER 7

"Hey daddy. Are you feeling ok?" I ask.

"Hey Bay-girl. I am." He says without a second thought. I look at momma and she smiles at me.

"Mom, how are you feeling? Are you ready for the big day?" I ask her.

"Yes. I am." She says. She seems to be feeling better. The color has come back to her face. I talk to them for a few more minutes about some of the details of the wedding so that they will know how to walk in, where to sit, and how to light the candles as they listen to me intently.

"Do you want us to send the photographer in to take pictures of you, or do you want to wait and go in the room with Sierra later this afternoon?"

"I'll wait."

"Ok. That's fine. I'll go tell her." As I exit the room, I hear Sierra crying only to walk into the suite to see Chandler with her hand on her left hip, standing over her as she scowls. I hope Chandler didn't take her ass in that room, upsetting Sierra about this mess.

"Chandler. What the hell is going on?" I ask.

"Nothing." She begins to relax her arm and the scowl on her face when she looks at me. Her eyes turn solemn.

"I'm sorry I wasn't a good big sister to you Donna," she says.

"What are you talking about?"

"You've been through two near-death experiences, watched our brother die, lost all of your money from your settlement, passed out over a t-shirt, and who knows what else and we just sat idly by, watching it happen; especially, Sierra." She looks over at Sierra who has now cowered in her chair.

"Don't you have something you want to tell Donna?" she asks Sierra.

"Look guys, whatever it is, it can wait. Come on Chandler, this is Sierra's wedding day. Why are we doing this?" I ask.

"A wedding *you* planned Donna, and Sierra has something to tell you. Don't you Sierra?" Chandler asks, sounding frustrated.

CHAPTER 7

Deciding that Chandler is not going to give up, I concede and ask, "Sierra. What do you have to tell me?"

"Daddy has a separate insurance policy for you. He got it shortly after you were born. I was being nosy one day and found the paperwork. I showed it to mom and she was so furious that she called the insurance company and put my name on the policy as the beneficiary and replaced yours then got one for Chandler. She said that I deserved it since I brought it to her attention. Then, on the family policy where all three of us were the beneficiaries, she removed your name and left mine and Chandler's. That's the one you knew about."

"...and what else?" Chandler pushes Sierra to continue talking.

"...and daddy doesn't know about your policy."

"Wow." I say. I never would have thought my own sister would have stabbed me in the back like this. But what they don't know, is that I bought a policy on mom and dad that I have been paying on for years. Dad knows, mom doesn't. I got it before I left Georgia and he helped me fill out the paperwork because it was his idea. I sit down on a chair and stare at Sierra and I can see my mom in her; full of greed and selfishness. Chandler walks over and sits beside me as I shake my head at Sierra in disbelief.

"Are you ok?" Chandler asks.

"I don't know. Like mother, like daughter I guess." I say, looking at Sierra before continuing, "Since I got here, there has been one bad memory after another. I'm kind of over it. I think the icing on the cake is that Sierra is keeping all of these secrets and assisting mom in her wrongdoing. I need some air." I stand up to walk away when Chandler shoots an ugly glance at Sierra.

"You aren't innocent in this either Chandler. I saw the look you gave daddy yesterday. You keep secrets too and I asked you to leave *this* alone but you just couldn't let it go."

"What are you talking about?"

"I'm talking about the way you and dad looked at each other before he walked out of the room yesterday after I passed out."

"We were just worried."

"Worried? Ok."

"You need to talk to dad."

"No. I don't need to do anything. I'm going to go in my room and gather my belongings so that I can go home after this wedding is over."

"You can't leave Donna," Chandler pleads.

"Watch me." My phone vibrates so I look down to see an important message from my boss. I have to call her so I walk out the room because she sent a message yesterday and I didn't respond. I step in the hallway as the phone rings.

"Donna, how are you?" Melanie asks.

"As well as can be expected."

"...and your mom?"

"Slowly declining. I got a message to call you."

"Yes. It's the weekend so we will have to wait until Monday to chat. I tried to reach you yesterday."

"Wait until Monday?"

"Yes."

"I am still on vacation so whether we talk today or Monday, it won't make much of a difference." I feel something in the pit of my stomach bubbling up. Something isn't right.

"I guess you're right. Well, I will give you a heads up and then we can discuss it formally on Monday. The company has decided to eliminate your position Donna. I'm sorry. We will talk more about it on Monday."

There it is, the bubble in my stomach is about to blow. I knew something wasn't right when I got that email and I felt it in my gut when she started talking. She has wanted me off her team since day one. I refuse to give her any power today and take the conversation in stride.

"Eliminated my position? Am I the only one who has been affected by this lay-off?"

"I can't disclose that information."

"Ok. Let's talk Monday." I hang up the phone. It's a good thing that I have

CHAPTER 7

a plan B. Honestly, I can't deal with any of this right now.

"You lost your job?" Chandler asks, startling me.

"Were you eavesdropping Chandler?"

I drop the phone on my bed and place my head in my hands. I knew it. That woman had it out for me so I knew it was as matter of time before she got rid of me.

"What time is it?" I ask.

"It's almost two o'clock."

"Ok. The rest of the vendors will be here in an hour."

"You can't change the subject Donna."

"I can and I did. But since you want to talk, what did you mean when you told me I needed to talk to dad?"

"Nothing."

"You sure? Let's just go and ask him." I walk out the room, Chandler trailing behind me, and call for dad to come into the hallway.

"What's going on? Why are you yelling?" asks dad.

"Chandler seems to think there is something you need to talk to me about. Care to share?" I ask.

Dad looks at Chandler who hunches her shoulders but doesn't say a word.

"What does she think we need to talk about Donna?" he asks. That means he is upset. He rarely calls me by my first name.

"I don't know. But, there seems to be a lot of secrets around here daddy. I'm getting tired of it. Did you know that mom found an insurance policy you took out for me after I was born and replaced my name with Sierra's?"

"Yes. I got a letter about it when I was updating some information. I changed it back."

"Ok. Why do you have a separate policy just for me?" I ask.

"That's a long story." After a brief pause, he looks at Chandler and asks, "Is this what you wanted me to talk to Donna about?"

"No," I intervene, "she told me to talk to you about the look you two

CHAPTER 7

exchanged yesterday in the room after I passed out."

"Donna. Let's talk about this after the wedding, once everything is settled and back to normal. Our emotions are all running high right now. We really need to sit down and talk about this. Ok?"

That's the second time he has called me by my first name in a matter of minutes. This must be really serious. I look at him and glance at my mother in the bedroom who is smirking at me. She thrives on chaos so this works for her. Before I can ask any more questions, the doorbell rings. No one is supposed to be here until three o'clock, so someone is early. Without a word, I walk away to answer the front door and I hear my dad whisper something inaudible to Chandler.

The world I have so carefully crafted, is coming down on me and I am losing control. My family is starting to aggravate me and I just want to get away. The one time I want to run, I can't and it's tough to admit that Chandler is right. As much as I want to, I can't leave after the wedding. "Keep it together Donna," I say aloud. I look through the peephole at the door to find that some of my cousins, along with an aunt, have arrived early and roll my eyes. They are just here to be nosy. I have a half a mind not to answer the door but my dad walks up behind me and asks who it is. Without saying a word, I turn and walk away. I will let him handle it. I head to the back yard once again, trying to get away from the madness and now I am back to square one. The mom is evil. One sister is greedy. The dad and oldest sister are keeping secrets. Am I the only one in this family who tries to be honest and do the right thing? After about two minutes, I hear cousin Rose call my name, "Donna!"

"Yes Rose?"

"I came out here to see if you need some help."

"I'm good, thanks. Sierra may need you inside." Rose means well but I can't deal with her right now. She is one of the few cousins I keep in contact with. She looks beautiful in her pink fitted dress. She pulled her hair into a messy bun in the top of her head with a few tendrils hanging down. She, too, has dimples. She is my dad's niece. Rose is about two or three inches shorter than me, and people say we look a lot alike. Looking at her today, I can really see the resemblance.

"You look beautiful today. Pink is a good color on you." I say to her.

"Thank you, cousin. I just threw this on to come help. I brought a silver dress to wear for the wedding. Are you alright?"

"I'm fine."

"I know this is short notice but would you mind being a hostess for the wedding? We didn't have time to ask someone on such short notice when we were planning, but a silver dress would be perfect to wear."

"I'd be…honored." Her southern twang in her voice is so cute and sincere. I thought my accent was noticeable but I've got nothing on her.

"Great. Let's go see what Sierra needs before the massage therapist comes."

She follows me into the house and we walk into the wedding suite. Sierra's eyes grow big when she sees Rose. She jumps up and runs to her and hugs her tightly.

"Rose," she says, "I haven't seen you in a couple of years. I'm so glad you made it to the wedding."

I take a mental note that Rose doesn't come around over here much either, which is surprising because my dad is her favorite uncle. Maybe her life is busier now that she lives in Atlanta. On a good day, it's almost an hour drive to Gainesville. I can just imagine what's it's like during peak travel times. I begin to back out of the room when I bump into Chandler, who'd strategically placed herself in the way so that I wouldn't be able to leave without notice. I make a mental note, "Check mark for Chandler." However, the look I gave her must have scared her because she scooted out of the way just as quickly as she moved behind me.

"Don't go Donna," Sierra says.

"I have a few more things to do," I lie.

CHAPTER 7

I don't want to be in her presence, and I am trying not to make it uncomfortable for everyone. I know that if I stay in the room with them, the tension will be so thick you can cut it with a knife. Once again, I am saved by the bell as the doorbell rings.

"I'll get that," I say as I head towards the front door. This time it's the massage therapist. She brought two more people with her, along with two extra tables saying Chandler requested them for the three sisters. The heifer was only supposed to get one for Sierra but this is actually much needed.

"Really?" I ask. I direct them to the wedding suite to set up and tell them I will be right back as I request Rose's assistance. Now I am glad she is here early. Her mom and sisters are in my parent's room, chatting away, so I give her the list of vendors.

"These vendors will be coming in to set up shortly. Can you take them to the tent and make sure they have what they need? I didn't know that Chandler called for additional therapists."

"Sure," Rose says.

"Thank you Rose." As I begin to walk away, the doorbell rings and a few more vendors show up. I take them to the tent and show them where to set up and Rose takes over for me from there. I walk back to the suite and ask the therapist what she needs me to do. Lord knows I don't want to get this massage, but I definitely need it.

It's good that the massage therapists came prepared. They had everything from scented oils to music for a relaxing mood. They even brought housecoats for us to keep and asked us to hand out their cards to people who would enjoy their services.

"We'll definitely have you back over soon. Dad will enjoy it and maybe you can do something to help mom relax." The card says they do a "gentle-touch massage." That'd be good for mom. It's almost wedding time. The make-up artist has arrived and is ready to do Sierra's make-up. To my surprise, she also has a second person with her so they can service me, Chandler, and my mom. "That is a nice touch Sierra. Check mark for you," I say to myself.

It's five o'clock and people are beginning to start pouring in. Rose is working overtime while helping everyone find their seats. The photographer was able to get some good shots of us while we were getting dressed, and we were able to take some pictures with some of the guys when we did a quick run through rehearsal after our make-up was done. Sierra said that she and Aaron had gone through a quick rehearsal with Aaron's uncle who is the officiant, so they know how everything will go and apparently Aaron talked to his cousin about all of the music to play. Sierra informed us that we will be walking down the aisle to an instrumental version of *Marry Me* by Train. As long as it's not ghetto, I don't care. She can do what she wants to do after she says, "I do."

There are a lot of people here so I'm glad we got a valet. Otherwise, waiting for everyone to park their cars would have been a mess. The system we used to take the cars in the back lot works well. They park and walk back to the front through a small opening in the gate.

The sun begins to set, the ambiance is perfect, Sierra is in her dress and ready to marry the man of her dreams. I tell Rose to close the doors and not let anyone in during the ceremony until after Sierra walks down the aisle. We don't want any distractions on the video. Chandler had some wedding programs made so I hand them to Rose because it's almost time to get this show on the road.

I line everyone up, and signal to Rose for the procession to start. When it's almost time for Chandler and me to walk, I open the door to tell daddy that it's almost time for him to walk out with Sierra.

The wedding is nothing short of magical. People are seated at their tables, snapping pictures, as we walk through. Sierra looks so beautiful that everyone takes a deep breath when she walks through the door. The band begins to play, "This Is Why I Love You" by Major and, to my surprise, Aaron starts singing to Sierra as she walks down the aisle. Sierra slowly walks towards him in a fitted,

CHAPTER 7

beaded, Mermaid-style silver dress with a beaded train, and she looks like a doll. By the time Aaron was done singing, there wasn't a dry eye in the house. Sierra was even struggling to keep herself from going into a full ugly cry.

As I watch them go through their vows, I can't help but pay attention to my mom and dad. My father is holding mom's hand ever-so-gently, and my mom has placed her head on his shoulder. She looks happy, peaceful, and they both look proud of Sierra.

The couple decided on a beautiful tribute for Sam to be performed during their nuptials and it is amazing. They then hand out special gifts, as Aaron gives mom and dad a rose and Sierra does the same with his parents. Ms. Lydia, Aaron's grandmother, is a part of a special lighting ceremony because she introduced them. She smiles as she kisses each of them on their cheek and wishes them a long life as they light the candle together.

Once the ceremony is over, we take more pictures, and then the waiters begin serving us. I'd arranged for them to have hors d'ouevres while we are taking pictures so that the guests won't get hungry or drunk since I'm paying for open bar. Laughter fills the air, and Sierra and Aaron are all smiles. She walks over to me and hugs me before we take a family picture.

"Thank you so much sis. You made this night so special for us." I smile at her, telling her that it isn't a problem when we are interrupted by some guests. I'm ready for this night to be over. Trying to put on a brave face when your mom is dying, your family is lying, and you've just lost your job is a lot to handle in one day and I am exhausted. It finally hits me, I lost my job on my day off.

As the night continues, I am not in the mood for niceties with Sierra's friends. I don't know them, they know Chandler, so I am the spectacle, just like last night. Shai put a bad taste in my mouth with all of those questions. All of her other friends have been hitting us with questions like, "Is this the sister that never comes home?" I think I have had enough, when some lady walks up to me and asks me why I never

CHAPTER 7

come home, as if it is her business. She even tries to scold me, telling me that now that my mom is sick, she wonders if I regret my choices. No. I actually don't. I'm starting to believe that a lot of conversations are being held about me, and they don't seem to be too nice. Little miss Sierra has some explaining to do. She isn't as quiet as I thought. I'm guessing that's why Shai felt so comfortable last night when *she* decided to grill me about why I don't come home. Sierra had to have told her a little more about my absence than she should have. Chandler is finally fed up with the rude questions and remarks, so when a lady who introduces herself as Estelle asks me how long I will be in Gainesville, she tells her off.

"I'm sorry. I was asking for a friend of mine who wants to see you," she says to me.

"Who?" I ask.

"Gail."

"Who is Gail?" I ask.

"She knew you when you were younger, I believe, I'm not sure. But, she has been trying to see you for a while now."

"Ok. I'll ask my parents about her. Forgive us, people have been rude all night. Chandler didn't mean any harm."

"It's ok," she says.

The lady walks off and Chandler gives me a funny looking smile.

"Don't let me forget to ask dad who Gail is. That was weird."

"I won't, and yeah...yeah, it was," she says as she walks away like something seems to be bothering her. I stand there for a few minutes attempting to look through the sea of faces to find Rose and thank her.

Now that the wedding is winding down, and people are beginning to leave, we are able to relax. Leave it to my family to want to take the flower arrangements with them. Rose is doing a good job of keeping them from doing so on her watch.

I'm exhausted and I just want to go to sleep. I grab my phone and look at the selfies I took throughout the night when I notice that Stephen sent a text. "Hey, I know you're busy," it says, "My plans have

CHAPTER 7

changed and I am leaving for Atlanta tomorrow."

"Are you busy?" I respond.

"No. Not at all."

I call him and after a couple of rings, he answers his phone, "Ms. Lady. How are you?"

"Hi Stephen. I am..."

"That doesn't sound good," he says.

"That's because it's not. The wedding was beautiful though."

"I can imagine."

"So you will be in the area tomorrow? For how long?" I ask.

"At least three weeks. Originally, I was supposed to come next Saturday and stay for two weeks."

"What changed?"

"They need help in the office and I am the only one who knows the job. My partner is out."

"What do you do? I know you have a business, but what does it entail?" I ask, realizing that I had never asked before because I didn't want to know. I didn't want to get too close.

"Business consulting."

"Ok. Nice."

"What do you do?" He asks.

"Well, I *was* working as a Regional Account Executive, but I just found out this morning that my job was eliminated. I have to call my manager back on Monday to get details about my severance and my next steps. I literally just got fired on my day off."

"I'm so sorry to hear that."

"Don't be. I always have a plan."

"That's good to know. But seriously, are you alright?"

"I will be. Thank you for asking. But this isn't about me, this is about you. I'm in Gainesville, about an hour away from Atlanta."

"Oh really? Maybe I can take you to dinner while I'm there?"

"Maybe. It'd be nice."

"Cool."

"Listen, I have to wrap up and make sure all of the vendors got paid. Sierra's send-off was beautiful. We had sparklers she and Aaron walked through them as they walked to their limo. She left me to tie up the loose ends."

"Ok. Call me later. But, I have one more question before you go."

"Ok. What is it?"

"Did she throw the bouquet?"

"Yes. It was the one thing I forgot to order, but Ms. Sherry, the florist, made one anyway."

"Did you catch it?"

"I thought you only had one more question?" I laugh and say, "To be honest, I wasn't even in the bunch Stephen."

"Hmmm…that's interesting. I thought all single ladies try to catch the bouquet."

"I'm not your average lady."

"I see."

"Ok. I will talk to you later. I've got to run."

"Good night."

We hang up the phone. Armed with all of the payment and tip envelopes, I run to catch the band manager as he heads towards the house. He seems pleased with its contents, shakes my hand, and walks away. I find the bartender, the valet team, and the caterer and hand them their envelopes as well. All of the guests have left the tent so I go back to turn off all of the lights, grab the box of leftover liquor, and prepare to lock it up. With no people inside, it has gotten cold in the tent but I sit down at a table anyway, not quite ready to go inside the house. Maybe I should get everything together for tomorrow's clean-up crew. After a few moments of contemplation, I stand up and start cleaning, glad that this night is over and that mom was able to see Sierra's big day.

-8-

That's My Daddy

I'm so glad that the wedding is over and everything is getting back to normal because my menstrual cycle has just started, I'm now upset with my sister, and I don't feel like being bothered. Sierra and Aaron have decided that they are going to go to Greece for their honeymoon, but are going to wait because of mom's worsening condition. Even though I know this isn't the case, I can't help but think about everyone planning their lives around the death of one person. It sounds kind of harsh to say you are going to wait until your mother dies before you go on a ten-day honeymoon vacation.

It always seems like, once the doctors tell people that they have a certain amount of time to live, they die soon after and I'm not sure if it is because they have given up on life, or if they are really just knocking on death's door. I believe my mom was worse off than they told me because she is deteriorating too fast. Either way, death seems to be taking its hold on my mother. She has stopped eating completely and didn't touch her food at the wedding. She has already planned her funeral, all the way down to the obituary that she won't let anyone see, except for my dad. It's disheartening. I have been sitting with her a few hours at a time to try to give my dad a break, but he won't leave her side. My mom has started asking me to hold her hand, or rub her back. She even asked me to comb her hair this morning. She never went through chemo so she still has a full head of hair, though not as thick as it once was. Her health has been on a rapid decline over the weekend, like she used all of her strength for the wedding.

It's Sunday night and Stephen has finally landed in Atlanta. His first call, it seems, is to me. I hear the footsteps and conversations of the other airplane passengers and, soon after, the hustle and

CHAPTER 8

bustle of the airport in his background as he waits for his luggage at the carousel.

"It's interesting that I had to travel all the way to Atlanta to finally see you again," he says.

"I know. I'm sorry. Life has a way of making you do what it wants."

"You can say that again."

I hear him grab his luggage as the wheels clink against the metal carousel. He begins to walk towards the car rental center, and I hear his breathing change as he tries to keep a quick pace, roll luggage, and handle the phone.

"Call me back once you get your rental car. It will be easier for you."

"Good idea. Please answer."

"I will."

About thirty minutes later, he gives me a call and tells me that he is headed to his hotel. I can tell he is extremely tired by the way he is dragging his words.

"Dinner tomorrow?" he asks.

"Sure. I think I'd like that."

"Great. After I finish up a few meetings, I should be free around four and I will head your way."

"You're thinking of coming all the way out here?" I ask in disbelief.

"Yes. I don't want to take you too far from your mom. I came this far, what's another hour?"

As he continues to talk and make plans, I think about how it's only an hour for him, but precious minutes to us as we care for mom. I'm glad he understands that.

"Thank you," I say.

"No problem. It will give us time to get to know each other and, you can bounce a few ideas off of me for your next business move if you'd like. Are you looking for other employment, or do you think you want to start your own business?"

"I'm exploring all options right now. I have a safe fund that I have been saving for about ten years, for rainy days like this. Starting my own business may be ideal right now since I will have my severance pay and benefits for a little while. We'll talk about it tomorrow."

CHAPTER 8

Having a rainy-day fund is a lesson I learned a long time ago, when mom screwed over me. That will never happen again.

I find myself anticipating our date tomorrow and I am getting a little excited about seeing him. But I still don't know where my life is going to take me, and until I figure out a plan for caring for my father, I don't know if it will include me remaining in Houston. Logically, I'm the best choice to watch over dad. Both of my sisters are now married. Chandler has a family, and I am sure Sierra will start one soon. I no longer have a job tying me down in Houston either. Aside from all of that, I miss my dad and the experience of watching my mom go through this, makes me love and appreciate him even more. Stephen and I talk over the next few minutes as he drives along.

"I just made it to my hotel," he says.

"Great. I'm glad you made it safely. I will let you get checked in and settled."

"Okay. I will talk to you tomorrow. I'm looking forward to seeing you again."

"I'm looking forward to seeing you too."

We say our good nights and goodbyes and I smile at the thought of getting to know him. He seems thoughtful.

After I hang up, I hear my dad yelling for the nurse so I run to the room.

"What's wrong?" I ask. I look at my mom, whose eyes have rolled in the back of her head and it looks like she is having a seizure. Nurse Petar made it to the room before me and is trying to stabilize her and make sure she doesn't bite her tongue. My dad is visibly shaken by the events. Chandler tries to calm him down while I pick up the items that fell on the floor. Water and ice are everywhere. I go to the bathroom and grab a big towel so I can wipe it all up. From the expression on Nurse Petar's face, it doesn't look like mom is going to be here very much longer.

I shoot Stephen a text, asking to postpone dinner. I can't leave at a time

like this. My father notices and asks me
who I am contacting.

"A guy friend of mine who just
flew into Atlanta."

"Guy friend? He came here to see
you? You never mentioned a guy to me."

"He's new dad and no, he didn't fly
here specifically to see me. He is here on
business. I'm letting him know that I can't
leave for dinner tomorrow like we'd
planned."

"Ask him if he'd like to come
here."

"No sir."

"Yes ma'am. I know you are
changing plans because you don't want to
leave me and your mother alone, so why
not?"

"Because I'm essentially inviting a
stranger to your house."

"You say that as if there weren't
over a hundred and thirty strangers here
yesterday. Neither you nor Sierra asked
me if *that* was ok and she certainly didn't
run that guest list by me."

"Sierra asked mom," I say, "But
you're right. We should've asked you. A

few people on the list you didn't want to see dad?"

"Perhaps. The point is that your friend is welcome to stop by and break bread with the family. Because if you like him enough to accept a date, you like him and ain't no man gonna fly all the way to Atlanta to be stood up."

"He didn't fly here for me, dad. He was scheduled to come here next week anyway."

"So he came early? Yes he did. He just told *you* that he had business. I guarantee you that you're his business. I'm sure whatever he had to do could've waited until next week."

"Ok dad. You've made your point. I will ask him to come over instead."

I send another text to Stephen, telling him about the condition of my mom and asking him if he'd like to come to the house, per my father's request. "I know it's bold to ask," I say, "Would you mind having dinner at my parent's house instead? My father insists."

CHAPTER 8

"Stephen responds with, "No problem. I truly understand the circumstances. I'll bring dinner and wine."

"That sounds wonderful but I can cook for us," I respond.

"It will take you away from caring for your mom and I don't mind."

He is sweet but now he is getting too close. I know that my dad is asking this of me because he wants to meet the guy who has managed to catch my attention, something that is not so easy to get. Once before my father told me that I shouldn't have sworn off men because of one bad apple so I'm sure this makes him happy.

My mom seems to be feeling better, and we end up reading to her for the better half of the evening. Dad is now playing her favorite song for her. He even put it on repeat for a couple of hours to relax her. Nurse Petar has started around-the-clock care, which isn't a good sign. I can see my dad's heart breaking a little more each hour as he works hard to try to keep mom comfortable.

EIGHT MOMENTS

Monday morning finds me anxious as I prepare to call Melanie. I say a quick prayer before dialing her number, asking God to hold my tongue and give me wisdom. I dial her number and she answers on the first ring.

"Hello Donna. Give me just a minute," she says.

Why is everyone, who never calls me "Donna" suddenly calling me by my first name?

"Ok. I'm back," she says as she begins to read this long letter about my dismissal. The company is basically giving me a six-month salary severance , I will remain on the payroll for two months, I will still get my bonus, and I will have to us those two months to find another job. An internal job search is mandatory in order to qualify for my severance package. All of my accounts will rollover to Tom, my current counterpart. I'm guessing that's why they brought me on board. They were giving me new accounts and wanted me to train my replacement in my specialty because he has no clue about what I do. The problem with that is, he isn't trying to

CHAPTER 8

learn it either. He is going to be in for a rude awakening. As far as me getting an internal job, this chick doesn't like me, so when I apply for another job in the company, I don't expect her to give me a good referral, especially since I wouldn't sign my year-end review because she inaccurately stated that I didn't meet a metric that I did, indeed, meet and had written proof from her to prove it.

"What are my next steps?" I ask.

"I will send you a few links and you can basically call today a work day, don't enter it as vacation time because you need to get this done today. Good luck on your endeavors. I will speak with you soon."

Did she just say, "Good luck?" This lady has lost her mind. Knowing that my mother is dying, she hits me with this news. I have about twenty more days of vacation time and I am going to take every bit of it to make sure that my family is ok.

I walk into my parent's room and sit in the corner, silently sulking like a little girl until my father asks me what's wrong.

"Nothing dad," I say, trying to fix my face.

"Did you talk to your boss?"

"Yes sir. I just finished talking to her. I have to go grab my laptop because I have to sign some paperwork. I will be on the payroll for two months and I am required to do a mandatory job search within the company in order to be eligible for my severance pay."

"So…you will get paid for at least eight more months?"

"Basically."

"Are you going to be ok?"

I look at him, wanting to tell him that I am *not* going to be ok. I want to sit in his lap and cry like a baby. I've dedicated several years of my life to this job for them to just throw me by the wayside with no regard for my health and welfare. Oh wait, I will still have health insurance at a discounted premium. But this still hurts very much. Melanie knows what I am going through but she still handled me with an "it's just business" attitude anyway. I kind of feel like she got a kick out of telling me that I will no longer be employed. I wish I could have reached through the phone and slapped her.

"I'll be fine daddy," I say, not knowing if I am really telling him the truth.

I walk to my room to grab the computer and decide to just stay there to fill out the paperwork. After I am done, I update my vacation time on the schedule and send an email to Melanie to let her know that I will be taking off for two more weeks because my mom's condition is worsening. Even though I don't say it, I have no intentions of doing any more work. I will not be checking email, nor will I be making any work-related phone calls for the rest of my *vacation* time in Georgia. They don't care about me so I have to care about myself and focus on my mom.

After a couple of hours, Stephen calls me to tell me that he is done for the day and he will head out in my direction before traffic becomes too bad.

"What would you like to eat?" he asks.

"I'm not sure. What do you have a taste for right now?"

"Italian, maybe?"

"Ok. You can go to *Yellowfin*."

"Ok can you text me the address and maybe some of the food items your family likes. Make sure you get enough for your sisters too."

"My sisters aren't here."

"Are they coming over?"

"They might."

"Then include them as well." I will be there soon.

Stephen is really trying to win me over and I don't know if I like this feeling or not. I think its sweet that he wants to make sure my family isn't hungry, but I feel kind of vulnerable and don't want that to cloud my vision. Aside from that, none of us have really had much of an appetite lately anyway. I look online and pick a few items out for the family to eat when I realize that they don't open until five. I call Stephen back to tell him.

"Hey Ms. Lady, are you trying to cancel on me again?" he laughs.

"No, I'm not cancelling. I was calling to tell you that they don't open until

CHAPTER 8

five o'clock. You should be here around four thirty, right?"

"Yeah, I'll be there around that time. I'll just find a liquor store to grab the wine and then head to the restaurant to order the food. Sound okay?"

"Sure. That will work. I'll send you the address." We hang up the phone and I send the address of the restaurant to him via text message. I guess I'll freshen up.

Heading to the bedroom, I hear my mom moaning and since she is in a lot of pain, I know my father is stressing. I knock on the door the check on them. He walks to the door instead of telling me to come inside, and for the first time, I see the woman who has always had this strange power over me in her most exposed state. I feel sorry for her.

"Mom, are you ok?" I ask.

Unable to speak, she just nods her head.

"Are you comfortable?" I ask her.

She shakes her head no.

Not knowing what else to ask, I walk over to her to try to make her comfortable but it seems like I am making it worse as she winces in pain. Maybe she shouldn't have been in that tent for that long at the wedding. Daddy grabs a few blankets he'd thrown in the dryer for her and began to wrap her with them to keep her warm.

"I ordered some food for you mom. Do you think you'll be able to eat it?" I ask.

"I'll try," she whispers.

Deciding not to add to the worry, I don't mention my employment woes. There is plenty of time for that. I look around to try to figure out what to do and finally settle on picking up a book. I sit on the floor beside her and start reading while my father looks on and smiles. No longer opting to go in the den at night to drink, he pulls out a bottle right in the room and begins to pour a stiff shot of José Cuervo gold tequila. Knowing how his day has been going, I guess it's a tequila kind of day. I take a break from reading.

"Stephen is on the way," I say.

Without a word, my dad pours a shot for me and holds it out for me to

CHAPTER 8

drink with him. Why does he have more than one cup in here? I grab the shot and we take our drink, both contemplating our lives in silence. After I sit there for a few moments, I finally decide to freshen up. I don't know how I feel, but I do know that I don't want to look thrown away. My daddy always says, "Make sure you always look like you came from somewhere. Don't go anywhere looking thrown away." The fact that he didn't say anything about my appearance when I told him Stephen was coming, let's me know mom is weighing heavily on his mind.

Stephen finally makes it to the house around six. He has to call a few times for me to give him directions to the house. He is dressed casually, but still looks very nice in his jeans and button-down shirt. I walk outside and he pulls me into a warm embrace. He smells so good, the kind of good that makes you want to stay snuggled in the embrace as your eyes roll back. I want to melt into him and stumble as I pull back to try to help him with the bags. He reveals that warm smile and makes me want to melt into a puddle of his goodness.

"Are you ok?" he asks.

Did he just ask me if I'm ok? Coming to my parent's house, looking and smelling like this, and he has the audacity to ask me if I'm ok. Nope. I'm intoxicated by the very essence of you. You sir, are a drug I am sure I don't want to try. But while I am thinking all of that, all I can muster up to say is, "Welcome to my parent's home."

"Thank you for having me. It's so good to finally see you again," he says.

If he could only read my thoughts. I am actually giddy about seeing this man, but too afraid to get out of my own way to tell him. I can admit that. I will never tell him but I can, at the very least, admit it to myself.

We walk into the kitchen and I give him a mini-tour of the house before inviting him to my parent's room for formal introductions, since my father made me promise to introduce him when he got there. I knock on the door and my father tells us to enter. My mom is sitting up, her

CHAPTER 8

hair combed to the side. She even put on a tad bit of lip gloss, to my surprise. Nurse Petar had to have helped her with that because I know my dad didn't.

"Dad, mom, this is Stephen." I say as we enter the room. My dad smiles and looks him up and down as if he is sizing him up.

"Nice to meet you Stephen," dad says.

"Likewise," Stephen says as he walks over to shake dad's hand. He looks at my mother who whispers a simple, "Hello Stephen." She looks at me and says, "He's very handsome Donna."

"Thank you," Stephen says while I stand there looking dumb-founded, blushing like a school girl with her first crush. Stephen doesn't notice as he chats away with my parents. Thank goodness for that.

After a little bit of conversation, the general routine of "who-are-you-and-who-are-your-people" conversation my father likes to have begins and Stephen obliges, finding out that my father actually does know some of his relatives that live here in Georgia. My father knows everybody.

Stephen and I walk back into the kitchen to eat and my father follows us so that he can get a plate for himself and mom.

"I can bring you a plate dad," I say.

"No. Enjoy your company," he says as he continues to make his plate. He decides against getting any wine and heads back to his room.

"Your parents are lovely," Stephen says.

"Thank you. I wish you were meeting them under different circumstances. It's kind of weird seeing my mom hooked up to a machine."

We settle in at the table, and he says a prayer before we eat without me having to ask. I find that impressive. Check mark for Stephen.

"You look nice Donna. Orange is a nice color on you," he says, referring to my orange shirt. When freshening up, I decided I wanted to be casual, without going overboard so I put on a burnt orange fitted top and some jeans. In this

CHAPTER 8

rare occasion, Stephen has already been exposed to one of my many quirks, my love of socks. I have on a weird pair of fuzzy, black socks with orange designs on them because they match my top.

"Thank you for the compliment. You look nice as well," I say.

We eat silently for a minute before he asks about my sisters and the wedding. I'm glad he brought it up because I do *not* want him to think weddings are on my agenda any time soon. I show him a few pictures in my phone and talk about the ceremony and how beautiful Sierra was.

"You organized all of this?" he asks.

"Yes."

"You did a great job. Maybe you should think about a career change."

"I don't know. I do a lot of these type of events with the non-profit I volunteer at in Houston when we are trying to do our fundraisers. I have considered it but don't know if I want to deal with fickle bridezillas. My sister was easy. Besides, if she'd started to get on my nerves, I would've just ignored her and kept doing what I was doing. I always know what's best." We laugh at the thought of that as he says, "Oh really? You *always* know what's best?" He shakes his head.

"You're going to be a handful, I see."

"Who me?" I ask playfully, "Never. I'm as meek as a little rabbit."

"Rigggggggghhhhhht…"

"I *am*," I say, pretending like I am trying to convince him.

"Ok," he says, "Where do you volunteer?"

"The H.E.A.R.T.S. organization for mothers who have lost their children to senseless murders."

"I've heard of that, the woman who started that lost her son in a police misunderstanding. Right?"

"If you call the police going to the wrong door, calling her a crack-whore, and shooting her son mercilessly a misunderstanding, then yeah."

"Wait. What happened?"

"Her name is JoAnn Whitmore. She and her son were home when the police came to her door just as her son, Taj, was leaving for the store. They ordered him on the ground and she heard the noise, so she opened the door to find out what was going on. The police then called her a crack-whore, telling her it was none of her business, a raucous ensued because they pushed her and her head hit the outside railing. Taj started questioning them, trying to find out what was going on because his mother was screaming in pain. By that time, the cops had him handcuffed. No Miranda Rights. No information about why he was being arrested. They didn't even try to find out his name. They suddenly started telling him to stop resisting, and one of them shot him four times. The impact of the bullets made him fall over the railing. They killed her son right in front of her eyes. To make matters worse, the guy they were actually after, showed up, killing one of the cops in the process in an effort to get away. He was killed on site. They tried to cover it up but a couple had it all on video and released the footage to the news."

"How do you know all of this?"

"I was there. I was driving through the area, trying to clear my head, when the shots rang out and I saw what they did to her. That's how we met. I helped her start the organization and now she is like a mother to me. Besides, the footage was all over the news."

"I remember that, now that you mention it. Wow."

"So, she created H.E.A.R.T.S. which stands for the Heal & Encourage A Renewal of Thy Self."

Stephen stares at me for a minute or so, seemingly impressed.

"Let's talk about something else," I say.

"Ok. I was going to ask you about the conversation you had with your boss today?"

"It was as I expected it to be. Two months on payroll, I have to look for a job within the company, and if I don't find a job, I will get a six-month's severance package."

"Ok. How do you feel?"

"Honestly, I feel jaded. I have given that company a lot of years. To get

CHAPTER 8

fired while I am here with my dying mother is a slap in the face, when I have sacrificed so much while working there."

"Are you going to be ok?"

"I'll be fine. I've been through a lot worse. Trust me."

He places his hand on mine and gently squeezes as he says, "It will be alright."

Chandler comes in the door and without looking up asks, "Whose car is that in the..." She stops mid-sentence when she sees Stephen.

"Chandler, this is Stephen," I say.

"Stephen. Nice to meet you. Wait, don't you live in Houston?" she asks.

"Yes. I'm here on business," he says, standing to greet her.

She looks him up and down before saying, "Business? Is Donna a part of this business?"

She is being a nosy, *extra* heffa right now.

"Actually, she is," he responds.

She looks at me and smiles one of those gone-girl smiles as she walks towards my parent's room.

"Don't mind her. She's the one who speaks her mind," I say after a few moments, thinking she has made it to my parent's room.

"Yes, I do," Chandler says, surprising us both.

"I thought you went to mom and dad's room?" I ask her.

"I did, I quickly peeked in to let them know I am here. But you're out of your mind if you thought I was going to stay cooped up in that room while you are out here with Luke Cage. You know I'm nosy."

I ignore her Marvel Comic reference because I know she was referring to his build and his height, and say, "Well, *Stephen* made sure that he brought enough food for you and Sierra so grab a plate and get some food."

"Thank you. I just talked to Sierra before I came in. She should be here any minute. I know she is going to love to meet you," she says to Stephen.

I can't believe she is acting like this in front of this man. I know I have been celibate, but I am not hard up for a man. I

CHAPTER 8

look at Stephen as he laughs along with my sister, taking her antics with a grain of salt and I like how comfortable he is with us, he seems really genuine. His smile is bright and he has relaxed his posture. Noticing my visual voyage of his body, he asks if I am ok. I embarrassingly blush and tell him I am fine. Crap. I can't believe I just got caught staring at him. I reach over to grab some more salad when Sierra walks into the house. She and I still haven't had much to say to each other since the wedding because I am still a little upset, and I don't really want to talk to her now. Before I can introduce Stephen, Chandler takes the opportunity to let Sierra know that I have a guest.

"Sierra, come meet Stephen," she says.

"Who is Stephen?" asks Sierra.

"Come see."

I sit silently and Stephen can tell something is wrong. When Sierra enters the room, she looks surprised but must have remembered me telling her about him, so she says, "Grocery store, right?"

"I call him Luke Cage," Chandler says.

Stephen looks at me, catching me playfully roll my eyes at Chandler and says, "I see you've been talking about me. Good things I hope."

"Of course," I say.

Sierra walks over and gives me a hug.

"We have food for you, if you're hungry. Stephen brought it," I say.

"Food? How nice of you Stephen," says Sierra. She walks over to him and offers him a hug as well and then says, "I want to go check on the parents first. Let me tell them I am here. Donna, can you come here for a second?"

I stand up slowly and walk towards her, telling Stephen I will be right back. I look at Chandler, "Don't run him away now. I know you don't do well with strangers." We all laugh and I follow Sierra into the hallway.

"What's up Sierra?" I ask.

She stops in front of our parent's door and says, "I want to apologize again and thank you for everything you did for

CHAPTER 8

the wedding. It was everything I wanted and more."

"You're welcome."

"Are you still upset with me?"

"Yep." I don't hesitate when responding because what she did was really messed up and low down.

"Donna, please don't be mad. Mom told me not to say anything and you know how persuasive she can be."

I look at Sierra, trying to figure out why she thinks this is an excuse. Out of everything she knows mom put me through, she is proving to be a mini-Dianne.

"Let me ask you something Sierra. What's up with Shai? Why was she grilling me so much about why I never come home? How did she even know?"

Sierra put her head down, "I was upset with you for not ever coming home and I always talked to her about it. She was out of line, but she knows about you and mom."

I don't believe that's all Shai knows but I don't want to keep asking her questions in front of our parent's bedroom door. I tell Sierra that I don't want to talk about it right now when dad opens the door.

"I hope you guys didn't think that we couldn't hear you," dad says.

"I'm sorry dad," I say.

I start to walk away so Sierra says, "Donna, don't leave." I keep walking. If mom heard us, then she is going to ask Sierra what we were talking about and that is a battle she will have to fight on her own.

"I'm sorry about that," I say as I walk back into the kitchen. Chandler looks at me, knowing that I am annoyed and says, "Stephen and I were just talking about you."

"Were you?" I ask.

Stephen says, "Yes. She told me about your high school days, when you used to work and save money while charging people to write their term papers for them."

"Yeah. I always have a plan B."

"I see. You told me that before. I love your drive Donna."

"Thank you."

CHAPTER 8

"Well…I'm going to leave you two to it. I need to go and make sure mom is ok and give dad a little break," says Chandler.

She stands up and takes her plate and glass of wine to the back with her.

"Are you sure you're ok Donna? Your mood changed a little when Sierra came in."

"I'm fine Stephen. I'm a little aggravated with her, but I'm fine."

We continue to talk for a little while longer, eating slowly and getting to know each other. I like how he pays attention to the little things and he isn't pushy when I don't want to immediately talk about something that's bothering me. Another check mark for Stephen. We finally start washing dishes, placing the food containers in the refrigerator for Sierra and head to the den to chat some more when I hear some chaos. Sierra calls for me to come to the room quickly so I jump up, Stephen in tow, to find out what the noise is about. I enter the room and see Nurse Petar trying to revive my mom and my dad holding her hand asking her to fight. Sierra is frantic and in the corner and Chandler is pacing back and forth.

"Did she have another seizure?" I ask until I realize my mom's heart monitor has flat lined. I stand there in horror, thinking the worst, when it starts beeping again. Everyone in the room takes a deep breath. After a few moments, she opens her eyes. My father kisses her. "We thought we'd lost you," he says. With all of us standing around her, she whispers, "I love you all." She looks at me and says, "Donna, it wasn't your fault." She closed her eyes and took her last breath. In shock, we all stand around her, waiting for her to say something else but she never does. Nurse Petar yells for one of us to call 911 and she continues to try to revive her.

Not knowing what to say to us, Stephen springs into action. When EMT arrives, he is the one who opens the door for the emergency crew and directs them to the bedroom where they try to take over the revival with no success.

"Time of death, 8:00 P.M." Nurse Petar proclaims.

CHAPTER 8

Dad falls over her in tears and I walk over to him to try to comfort him. But, how do you ease a broken heart?

I don't know what to do. My family is in shambles and I am trying my best to help keep us all together.

Tearfully, I say, "I'm so sorry you had to witness this Stephen. I will understand if you need to leave."

"No Donna. I'm fine. I'm here," he says.

"But you didn't come here for this." A rush of emotions begins moving through me like a raging river and I don't know whether I want to cry, scream, or yell and Stephen knows I am a mess, trying to keep my composure. He walks over to me, hugs me tightly and my body involuntarily tenses up. He notices but he won't let go until I finally relax and melt into his chest in tears. I just lost my momma and I don't know if I'm hurt because she's gone, or relieved that she can't torture me anymore. Maybe it's a combination of both. What I do know is that Stephen is getting too close, too fast, and I am fighting it and just like this hug, he just won't let go so easily.

EIGHT MOMENTS

The night is hard on us. I can hear my father's sobs and I don't know what to do. Stephen stays as long as he can, but has to go back to his hotel room to get ready for his meetings tomorrow.

"I don't want to leave you like this," he says.

"No, I understand," I say to him. My face feels stiff and is covered in dried tears. I'd just planned a wedding, I'm not ready to plan a funeral, at least not *this* funeral.

"I will be back tomorrow morning. I have an important meeting at eight and then I'm going to cancel and reschedule everything else."

"Stephen, no. We will be fine."

"I insist," he says, "I won't take 'no' for an answer."

I nod in agreement, not wanting to argue with him and appreciating the concern. My sister's husbands both made it over before the funeral home picked up mom's body. Chad left my niece and nephew with his parents. Everyone is trying to grasp the fact that mom is gone, including me.

CHAPTER 8

I walk to my parent's room and see my dad sitting in his chair, staring out the window so I decide to leave him alone. As I walk away from the door, he calls me back.

"Come sit with me," he says.

Without a word, I sit on the floor beside him and we both stare out the window, watching the light of Tuesday morning overtake Monday night's darkness.

I awaken to the smell of bacon, biscuits, eggs, pancakes, and sausage. Who is up cooking this early in the morning? I must have fallen asleep on the floor. I look up and see dad is nowhere in sight. I slowly stand, gazing at the time. It's already almost twelve in the afternoon. I head to my room and grab my toiletry bag and some fresh clothes and chug along to the bathroom to jump in the shower. My goal is to be quick, but as the water falls on my body, I feel like it is washing all of my pain away. After a few moments, I decide to get out and hurriedly put on my clothes, brush my teeth, and finger comb my hair. I shuffle into the kitchen, telling everyone that Stephen will be coming back and bump right into him.

"Good afternoon sleeping beauty," Stephen says. He is standing at the stove, making a plate for himself while everyone else is at the breakfast table, eating in silence.

"I didn't realize you were here. No one woke me up. Good afternoon."

"I know you had a long night. I've only been here about twenty minutes." He walks over and hands me a plate of pancakes and kisses my forehead. I stare blankly, then look over at my family. My father smirks while still looking at his plate but never looks up. Sierra and Chandler are staring at us but don't say a word. Not knowing how to handle this situation, I thank him and walk to the table. Stephen joins me, grabs my hand, and begins to whisper a prayer. We all eat without saying a word, still shell-shocked.

As the day progresses, I realize I need to jump into gear. I email Melanie to tell her the news so that she can adjust my schedule accordingly. She gives me extended bereavement pay, the least she can do after firing me. I don't expect more from her, but it'd be nice if she shows a little concern. Shortly after I reach out to her, Tom calls me. I send him to voicemail. I'm not ready for any of his fake condolences. He leaves a voicemail message, asking if there is anything he can do to help and asks me to keep him informed about the funeral. His calls are followed by several of my other team members who were also sent to voicemail. I don't trust them and don't want to talk to them. In fact, let me get this straight, the company forced me off my job, the announcement was made and no one on the team called me. My mother dies and now they show concern? They can do a lot of things for me, but showing me fake concern is not one of those things. Since my mother has already planned out her funeral and written her obituary, I try to tie up the loose ends she may have left behind but my dad won't let me.

"I've got it Bay-girl. She wanted me to take care of it. I will take care of it," he snaps at me.

EIGHT MOMENTS

I'm trying to be helpful but I guess I'm getting in the way. Planning a funeral is so final. Sierra and Chandler were closer to her than me so they decide to take the lead in getting dad to let them help. I feel helpless. After several unsuccessful attempts, I back away. Stephen has his computer and is working in the den and invites me to come sit with him. He knows something is wrong.

"Let's get some fresh air," he says.

"I uh…"

"You don't want to leave your family?"

I shake my head.

"Let's just walk up the street."

"Ok," I say.

I grab my light jacket and some shoes and we walk out the front door. I take in the fresh air, the flowers, and the calm peace that you don't find in the city. I even think I smell honeysuckles in the breeze. I close my eyes and listen to a woodpecker peck away and I'm taken away to a place where only happiness exists. As another cool breeze rustles through the trees, it sends a chill through me. I shiver

CHAPTER 8

and Stephen puts his arm around me, pulling me closer to him, reminding me of my dad. He looks at me playfully, trying to cheer me up and says, "You know this means we go together, right?" I laugh.

"I'm just kidding," he says.

"I really appreciate everything you have done. I'm a complete stranger to you," I say.

"I'm here because I want to be, and if nothing ever comes of us, I will always be here for you."

We continue to walk as I contemplate what he's just said. He understands that my life is beautifully chaotic right now, but he really has no idea who I am. I wish we could skip this part, this awkward phase of getting to know each other, which has now been complicated by the death of my mother, an event he had the unfortunate burden to witness. We continue to walk, talking and finding a connection within each other. Our pace is slow, not too many expectations, just a comfortable space and I'm glad he understands.

EIGHT MOMENTS

We finally make it back to the house a couple of hours later and I feel better. But my nervous energy returns as soon as I walk back into the house. The air is thick, stuffy and the stench of death still lingers within. I don't know why I didn't notice it this morning when I woke up. I immediately feel nauseous and run to the bathroom. It finally hit me that my mom died in this house and that is yet another reason to never want to come back here. After regaining my composure, I slowly walk towards the den. Sierra and Chandler are getting ready to leave to go to the funeral home so I get ready to go with them and Stephen heads out to his hotel room.

"You need to spend this time with your family," he says, "I just wanted to make sure you were alright. Keep me posted." Just like that, he's gone.

The funeral will be held Saturday, which is enough time for all of the family to come in from other states. We picked out a white casket, per my mom's request, and make additional arrangements for her flowers and burial site. Mom had already paid for her funeral, she knew exactly what she wanted, and she'd arranged for a lawyer to execute her will.

"I guess she thought of everything," dad says.

"I guess so," says Chandler. I decide to keep quiet. We make it back to the house and I continue to be silent as they all rummage through her things, looking for items she specifically requested to wear at her funeral. I feel out of place and they don't need me.

Over the next few days, guests begin to drop by to offer their condolences. Women are coming over with food and plates, high skirts and low-neck lines; leaving their numbers for my father to give them a call if he *needs* anything. One woman was bold enough to just say, "I'm lonely and I need someone to comfort me at night." When she left, I made sure I threw her spaghetti dish, and her number, in the trash. I don't trust it. When I told him what I'd done, Stephen laughed at me and told me I was wrong.

"No Stephen, *she* was wrong," I say, "My momma hasn't even been put in her grave yet!"

"Are you ready for tomorrow?" he asks.

"No. I don't think anyone can ever truly be ready to bury a parent. But, I am doing the best I can," I say.

"That's all anyone can ask."

"Are both of your parents alive?"

"Yes."

"Have you talked to them since all of this has happened?"

"Yes. I called them Monday night after I left here."

"Are they ok?"

"They are doing well. Since they are both retired, they do a lot of traveling."

"That sounds nice. I definitely would love to do that once I retire. I want to travel the world," I say.

"Me too. I'd love to travel and learn about other cultures, maybe have a home somewhere that I can go to as a getaway from the hustle and bustle of life."

"That sounds nice."

CHAPTER 8

"What are your plans for tonight after the viewing Donna? Would you mind if I come by and spend some time with you?"

"No. I don't mind. I actually feel like I am in the way and they don't need me here."

"Why do you feel like that?"

"Because, I haven't been home in twelve years. My mother and I, well, we never really got along." I start to feel tears well up in my eyes.

"Didn't get along? Really? So how did you see your family?"

"It's a long story but, we either met up for some type of family vacation that my mom always found an excuse not to join, or my dad and sisters would come see me in Houston. Are you sure you want to stop by tonight? It will be late."

"I will be there at about nine or so and I got a hotel room about ten minutes from the house for tonight and tomorrow so I can be closer to you."

"You did?"

"Yes. We can talk about everything tonight. Ok?"

"Ok Stephen."

We hang up the phone just in time for me to answer the door for another visitor. This one is just completely out of line.

"Is Mr. Catchings home?" she asks.

"Yes. He is," I say.

"I'd like to speak to him please." She adjusts her tight fitted black pencil skirt. She has on four-inch stilettos and a button down fitted top with her bosom bursting out. She has on a little make-up and she is very attractive and shapely. Every hair on her head is in place. She peeps in the house to look around for my dad as I invite her into the den.

"Have a seat. What's your name?" I ask.

"Debbie," she says, handing me a large Tupperware container. "I brought dinner for the family." She takes a seat on the couch and crosses her legs at the ankles. She seems nice but I don't like her and I know she's just sniffing around the house, trying to find a bone.

"I'll be right back Debbie. I will check to see if he is available."

CHAPTER 8

I walk to my parent's room and ask dad if he is interested in visiting with people.

"Who is here Bay-girl?" he asks.

I want to tell him that some hussy is here to try to feed him, sleep with him, marry him, and eventually try to take all of his money but I just say, "A lady by the name of Debbie."

"Debbie? Debbie who?"

"I don't know. I can tell her to leave, if you'd like."

"No. I'll go see who this is."

We walk back to the den and she jumps up and walks towards him, wrapping her arms around his neck.

"Hi Gabe. I came by to check on you." Her tone is flirty as she takes her right pointer finger and runs it down his chest. She bats her eyes, and her fake eyelashes are so long, I would have thought she would have flown away. He pulls back, grabbing her arms to try and push her away.

"What are you doing here Debbie? Is there something in your eye?" he asks.

I want to laugh but I'm puzzled because he actually knows her.

"I came to check on you and make sure you have everything you need."

She takes that same finger, showing off her perfect French manicure, and places it in her mouth. I have just about had enough of these shenanigans.

"Debbie," I say, "Do you not see me standing here?"

"Oh. I'm sorry. I wasn't paying attention," she says snidely.

"Well, my mother hasn't been buried yet, and if you want to keep those perfectly manicured nails on your hands, and your hair in place, you might want to think twice about flirting with my dad in front of me." I cross my arms to let her know I mean business.

"Your mom? Wait, who are you?"

"She is Donna, Debbie, and you are out of line," my father says.

He walks to the door and opens it saying, "I'm going to have to ask you to leave and don't ever come back here again."

CHAPTER 8

She looks at me and back at him and slowly walks out the door. My father slams it behind her and looks at me.

"You don't know who that is?" he asks me.

"No."

"That's your momma's friend."

"What? No. Ms. Debbie, her friend from work?"

"Yes."

"She looks different."

"I guess. Maybe it's just because you haven't seen her in years."

"I can't believe she came over here like that."

"Death sometimes brings out the worst in people baby."

As he walks back to his room, he shakes his head.

The viewing is tonight at six and no one in the family is ready to go, especially me. I haven't been in a funeral home since Sam died and momma told me she should have let her cousin kill me. To tell the truth, I'm a little scarred.

"Are you guys ready to go?" asks dad.

"I'm ready," Chandler says and Sierra and I just fall in line. We walk to the car and file in, one after another, like we used to do as kids. Dad turns the car on and waits for Chad and Aaron to do the same so that we can follow each other.

"No one wants to sit up here with me?" dad asks.

"I do," I say. I didn't want to sit next to Sierra anyway. I jump out the car and get in the front passenger seat next to daddy and we head to the funeral home for the viewing. Thank goodness it is only an hour long.

The funeral director has done a wonderful job ensuring all of mom's requests are in place, all the way down to her hair. Several friends and family stop by to see her and offer their prayers and condolences but I don't notice many of them as I stare at my mother's lifeless body. She looks as if she is sleeping peacefully and her makeup is flawless. She has on a white dress and a beautiful brooch that matches her earrings and the sparkles easily catch your eye. I'm sure she knew

CHAPTER 8

that when she requested it so that all eyes will be on her at the funeral.

After the viewing, my father seems to be in better spirits, "Dianne looked beautiful, didn't she?" he asks during the drive back to the house.

"Yes," Sierra says.

"She looked at peace," says Chandler.

I keep my mouth closed and feel all eyes on me.

"Donna, don't you think she looked beautiful today?" daddy asks.

"Yes," I respond.

We drive for a few minutes in silence when Sierra finally asks, "Donna, why won't you let it go? She is dead now and you are still holding on to the pain."

Sierra is the last person who can give me some advice. I roll my eyes as I continue to stare out the window but don't answer her. My father grabs my hand and gives it a little squeeze and then lets it go to turn on the radio.

"I know you heard me Donna," Sierra says.

Daddy turns the volume down and asks, "What's wrong with you two?"

"Nothing daddy," I say.

"She's mad at me because I didn't tell her about the life insurance policy," says Sierra.

"That's not why she's mad," Chandler interjects, "She is mad because of the way you handled it. Donna has never cared about money like that because she has always been able to make her own. You were wrong."

My father looks at them both through the rearview mirror and shakes his head.

"Donna, are you going to be alright?" he asks.

"I'll be fine daddy. I always pull through," I say.

We drive along for the next few minutes in silence, until dad turns into the driveway.

"Stephen is on his way," he says.

"How do you know?" I ask.

"Because I sent him a text to let him know we were headed home before we left the viewing.

CHAPTER 8

"You have his number?" I ask.

"Yes. I asked him for it yesterday."

Sure enough, while we were exiting the car, Stephen turns into the driveway.

"Perfect timing," dad says.

Stephen hops out the car and walks towards me with food, a bottle of wine, and his computer bag so I walk over to help him. As I grab the food and wine, he smiles.

"Look at you, always grabbing for the food," he jokes.

"I was trying to grab the first thing I saw," I say, laughing with him.

He leans in and kisses my forehead and we head towards the house.

"How are you doing Mr. Catchings?" he asks as he shakes my father's hand.

"I'm good Stephen, and you?"

"I'm doing well. I didn't know if you guys were hungry so I brought food," he says as he hugs Chandler and Sierra and shakes their husband's hands. Turns out everyone was starving so the food was right on time as everyone thanks him while washing up. We all begin to grab plates.

"Stephen, thank you for being here for us," I say.

"No problem Donna. Where shall we sit?"

"It's crowded in here, let's go in the den."

We walk into the den and get settled with TV dinner tables and, in true Stephen form, he begins to pray. This time, he not only blesses the food, he asks for peace within my family.

"Donna, I like you a lot. I know the circumstances are not ordinary, but I think that is what makes it so special," he whispers.

"I like you too. I have so many issues that you've not yet seen though, it scares me."

"Talk to me. Tell me why you haven't been home in years."

"It all started when I was nine," I say, "My brother Sam died while trying to save my life and my mother never forgave me for it."

"Ohhhhh. Ok, that's what she meant."

CHAPTER 8

"Yeah, she was saying that it wasn't my fault that Sam died. But it took her years to tell me that and she mistreated me most of my life because of her feelings about it."

I look at him, trying to see if his eyes will show signs of disinterest. Instead, he seems to be more intrigued.

"Donna, it's ok. Life happens like that sometimes. You just have to roll with the punches and you seem to have mastered that pretty well."

"Stephen, my mother hurt me in ways you can never imagine. Maybe one day I will tell you about it."

"Tell me about it now. You can't always be strong. Sometimes you have to tap out and let someone else get in the ring and fight for you."

I get up and walk to my room, telling him I will be right back. I open my suitcase and pull out the t-shirt Sam gave me and walk back towards the den.

"You see this?" I ask as I hand it to him, "This is my favorite shirt. I know for a fact that I packed this shirt when I got ready to leave because Sam gave it to me

EIGHT MOMENTS

before he died. Everyone knows how much I love this shirt so I was devastated when I got to Houston and couldn't find it. I was hysterical, combing through every inch of the boxes, and suitcases, I had. I called this house for months, asking everyone to help me find it. No one ever could. Surprisingly, when I got here, it was in the bedroom chest-of-drawers in my old room, a room that has been practically untouched. I later found out that my momma gave it to Sierra to put in my drawer before I got home, supposedly so I could find it. There are a few things wrong with the story. Momma always said she didn't know where it was, so how did she have it to give to Sierra to place in my drawer? The second thing is, it wasn't on top of anything, I found it because I got a bit of nostalgia and started sifting through my old clothes. That says to me that I really did pack it like I originally thought, and she took it out and purposely hid it after she told Sierra to put it up for me."

You think she'd do that Donna?"

"Yes. I do, because she's done worse."

CHAPTER 8

"Like what?"

"Let's talk about it another time. Her funeral is tomorrow and I don't want to go in there with ill feelings. I will say this, when she passed away, I don't know if I was more relieved because she can't torture me anymore, or hurt because she is gone and feeling this way is not a good feeling."

"Donna, it will be ok. You are entitled to feel any way you like. They are your feelings, no one else can tell you how to feel."

I look at him and can't control my emotions as tears start to fall. He stands up and moves the TV tables away from us, reaching out for my hand. I take it and stand up, though I really don't want to, and he pulls me into another one of those bear hugs to let me cry again as he sways back and forth with me. I know he is wondering what he has gotten himself into.

Momma's funeral is packed with people I haven't seen in years and a lot of the people from Sierra's wedding are here to offer their condolences. I am numb. I don't know a lot of these people and I don't like funerals. Maggie and JoAnn both flew in from Houston to show their support, but I knew they would. I can always depend on them to be there when I need them. I see them in the middle section and they smile when they realize I am looking at them. I am happy they are here. I continue to look around at the sea of black dresses and suits and recognize a few other faces when I see Estelle sitting quietly in the back, right corner. Stephen walks in and, coincidentally, sits next to her. He nods at me when he realizes that I see him. I have to hand it to him; the man looks good in a suit and going out of his way for me has really made an impression. I bet he smells good too. Check mark for Stephen.

Flowers are everywhere and the air smells like sweet tears on a hot midsummer's night. The room is warm from all of the body heat and heavy breathing that usually accompanies crying. My dad and sisters sit beside me on the front pew with my niece and nephew. Aaron and Chad, Sierra and Chandler's husbands respectively, are standing at the door,

CHAPTER 8

handing out the obituaries mom created. Dad said that she left off a few things, so he updated it before taking it to the print shop. I look down at my copy and see that my mother did not want anyone to speak out of turn. She wanted a few scriptures, a song, a tribute, and a eulogy. That's it. She wrote, "The family understands that Dianne was loved, cherished, and honored by many and appreciates your thoughts. We ask that you not express them at this time."

My father is so distraught, he probably can't sit through the funeral any longer than he has to, and I am sure my mom took that into consideration. Being here reminds me of Sam's funeral, once again. We were in the exact same church for his eulogy and I get an eerie feeling that something isn't right. I slide over in the pew to get closer to dad, just like I did when I was a little girl. When my mother's eulogy begins, the pastor's recollection of my mom and her contribution to the community is very moving and so believable that even I almost bought into it. I wonder if she wrote that too. He didn't speak very long, and he gave the family a Bible after he prayed over it. After everyone lined up to view momma one last time, we all left the church to head to the burial site. Stephen falls in line with me as we walk out the door, and grabs my hand. He walks us to the limo and tells me that he will be right behind me as it begins to rain.

The burial site is wet and cold and it is beginning to rain heavily so a lot of people decide not to come close to the mud. We watch as people throw flowers on the casket while they slowly lower it into the ground. I hurt for my father and don't know how to comfort him as he sobs silently. My sisters walk back towards the limo, leaving me and daddy behind. As they begin to throw dirt on my mother's casket, I say, "Goodbye momma." People begin to leave, but my father just stands there and I stand right beside him. Once everyone has gone, he breaks down, nearly falling to the ground. I hold onto him tightly, repeating Stephen's words, "It's ok daddy. I've got you. Sometimes you have

CHAPTER 8

to tap out and let some else get in the ring and fight for you."

Stephen notices that I am trying to walk through the mud with daddy and comes to help me get him back to the limo. Chandler is comforting her children and Sierra is crying uncontrollably. I guess that's why they didn't notice daddy's breakdown.

We finally make it to the repass, and I am starving. Stephen decided not to come and asked me to call him once the family has settled at home. He said he has some work to catch up on, which I completely understand.

After people begin to leave, my dad finally tries to eat the food on his plate, a luxury he didn't get initially because people were trying to talk to him and offer their condolences. I notice my sisters are huddled together and begin to whisper when they see Estelle who, once again, is hanging around. I need to know who this woman is and why she is here. Sierra and Chandler help usher people out so I finally take my opportunity to ask about Estelle.

"Dad, who is Estelle?" I ask.

"Estelle? I don't know. Why do you ask?"

"She was at the wedding, and she has been hanging around here today. At the wedding, she made it her business to tell me that one of her friends wants to see me, but she didn't mention it today, she actually didn't even speak, as if she was trying to avoid you. She just spoke and kind of kept her distance. But the friend she mentioned at the wedding, the one she said wants to see me was a lady named, Gina? Gloria? No, that's not right." I pause for a few minutes and the name finally comes to me. "Her name is Gail." As soon as I say the name, my dad spits out his food and jumps up. He grabs my hand and pulls me into the nearest hallway.

"She mentioned Gail?" He asks.

"Yeah. Who is she, and why does she want to see me?"

My father places his head in his hands.

"Sit down Bay-girl, it's time we have that talk I promised you."

I sit down, trying to understand why mentioning someone's name would

CHAPTER 8

cause this type of reaction from him. He begins to speak, "A long time ago, before you were born, I met a lady named Gail."

My daddy pauses for a long time, like he is struggling with his words. "She and I had been friends for years. I knew her before I married Dianne. We actually dated for a few years in college, but it didn't work out because I wasn't ready for the type of relationship she wanted."

I look at my daddy strangely, trying to figure out why he is telling me this.

"About a year before you were born, I saw her again. She'd moved to Atlanta and reached out to me to meet up for drinks. Dianne and I were having a lot of problems, I had one too many drinks, and Gail and I, well, we...had an affair."

Tears begin to form in his eyes as he struggles to tell me this news. "It was a mistake, but I couldn't stop going back to her and it went on for about six months."

I stare at him, not knowing what to say and still trying to understand what all of this has to do with Estelle as he continues, "Your mom found out and told me to break it off, but I couldn't. I was addicted to Gail, we did things that your mother never dreamed of doing. But…it was tumultuous at the same time. Gail was my dangerous escape until she got pregnant, and our lives changed."

"You had an affair daddy?" I asked, dumbfounded.

"Yes, with Gail and when your mom threatened to leave with your sisters and brother, I realized how much I love my family and couldn't continue to hurt her. I told Gail that it was over, not knowing that she was already pregnant and didn't hear from her for months afterwards."

"You have another child daddy? Where did you take the child?"

He takes a deep sigh before saying, "Gail dropped a baby off at the house with a note. That said, no one else will want me with four kids and that the baby belongs to me. She attached the birth certificate and the baby's name was Donna." I gasp and jump away from the table.

"Did she leave me with you or did she leave me on the doorstep?" I ask.

CHAPTER 8

"She waited until I opened the door, handed you to me, and walked off. I never heard from her again."

"So, you're telling me that I am a product of an affair? Dianne wasn't my mother and you let her treat me like trash because of your guilty conscience?"

"No. Yes. You look a lot like Gail. Dianne couldn't stand it because you were a constant reminder to her of when I stepped out."

I pace back and forth as I try to digest this news. I'm hurting, my breathing becomes staggered like a song in staccato as daddy sits there looking pitiful.

"Does Chandler know?" I ask

"Yes."

"...and Sierra?"

"No."

"Are you sure? You're telling me that Chandler knew, all this time and didn't share it with Sierra?"

"No. Chandler just found out recently when Gail approached her about six months ago, looking for you. If Sierra knows, it's because Chandler told her."

"Six months?" I ask as I begin to cry.

I guess I can understand why they kept it from me, how do you tell someone that their whole identity is a lie? The world that I have come to terms with has just fallen apart in a matter of seconds. Here I am, with mommy issues, trying to understand why she never loved me, only to find out that it is because I wasn't hers to love. It makes sense now, why she resented me when Sam died. She never wanted me in the first place. Still I ask, "What are you saying daddy?"

He looks weary and pulls a letter out of his wallet and hands it to me. I am puzzled as I look at the envelope, seeing the hand-written address deliverable to Gabe and Donna Catchings. I look at my daddy who then pulls a piece of paper with a number on it out of his wallet. The letter is from Gail and it simply says, "I've been looking for you Donna. It's time you know."

After a long pause, he continues, "When your mother found out about the affair I was having with Gail, it was a hard

CHAPTER 8

pill for her to swallow, and she spent the rest of her life punishing me for it through you."

My whole life has been a lie. Here I am, admiring my parents for the love they share, thinking that I want that type of love, only to find out that they aren't the happily married couple I thought they were, at least not in the beginning.

"So, daddy, I'm just trying to wrap my head around this. You're saying to me that the reason you let her treat me the way she did was out of guilt?" I figure if I keep asking, I will get an answer that I can understand but he doesn't answer.

"Is this the reason why you feel like her death is your fault? You think you drove her to drink?" I ask but he still doesn't respond. After a few moments, I say, "This is what you thought I was talking about in the bedroom. You thought mom told me? And, when Chandler and I approached you after I passed out in the room, you thought I knew because *she* knew?"

He finally musters up the strength to say a simple "yes."

EIGHT MOMENTS

"I thought the grass was greener on the other side until my back was pressed against the wall Donna. Dianne was the love of my life and we worked through the pain I caused her. I never should have stepped out on her and I should have protected you. This number belongs to your birth mother. She is waiting on you to call her." I look at his extended hand and stare at the number of the woman who abandoned me at birth to get even with my daddy because she couldn't have him. She didn't even have enough courage to come and find me herself, just sent a friend and I don't know if I want to get to know her. Life is forcing me to accept a new beginning. Damn.

-Epilogue-
Dianne's Side
of
Things

The truth of the matter is that Donna really didn't deserve the way I treated her after Sam died. I remember when she was born, a winter baby who forced her way into this world, and our lives, on December 12. I wasn't happy about it, mainly because of the circumstances that surrounded how she came to be. I loved Gabe with every drop of blood that flowed through my body. To learn that he was sharing himself with Gail, hurt me to my soul. The night I saw him with Gail was one I would never forget because it changed our lives forever.

It was a dark and gloomy night. Chandler, Sierra, and Sam were sick, and it was raining heavily. The night winds were howling, shaking the windows, competing with the song the rain made as it tapped a song of its own on the window panes.

Gabe was supposed to be out with his brother. The house phone rang that evening at around seven thirty and I quickly answered to keep from waking the sleeping children.

"Hello," I said.

"Do you know where your husband is?" a woman's voice asked.

"Pardon me?" I asked.

"Do you know where your husband is?" she asked again.

"Who is this?"

"Your husband is at 5-7-3-3 SW 8th place with Gail."

The voice hung up the phone, never telling me her name. My guess, a scorned woman who was upset that Gabe wasn't with her. So, what did I do? What every wife with sick kids would do in the middle of a storm, I packed up the kids and drove over to the address.

My heart sank when I saw Gabe's car, but I needed to see it with my own two eyes. I left the kids in the car, got out in the rain, and I walked around, peeping through windows, until I saw him passionately kissing her as they made love.

EPILOGUE

I stood there, watching, waiting for him to look up at me for at least five minutes. When his gaze finally caught mine, he began shaking and so did I; from the anger that started to well up in me as I walked to the front door. I don't know why, or where I got the strength, but I just started kicking the door in with all of my might, trying to break it down. Gabe came barreling towards me, trying to stop me from getting to Gail, and I slapped his ass so hard that the force made me slip and fall down on the wet floor. He was right though. My beef wasn't with her, it was with him.

"Why would you do this to me? To us? Why would you do this to our family?" I screamed at him before I ran away. He followed me with nothing on but his underwear and stopped dead in his tracks when he saw one of the three little faces looking up at him. Sierra. Knowing he was defeated, he stood there, dripping in the rain, looking stupid, not knowing if it was safe for him to stay or come home.

But I didn't leave him. A part of me wanted to take the kids and get a small apartment I could afford, never to return to his lying, cheating ass. Through all of that hurt and pain, I really wanted my husband and I really wanted my family. I started to question myself and I felt like I'd done something wrong to make him stray, to make him want to be with that whore. I wanted him to tell me that everything was ok and apologize. But, I also wanted to kill them both.

After that embarrassing episode at Gail's house, I decided to do a little digging and found out that the affair had been going on for months and when I confronted him about what I'd learned, he promised that he would leave her, even begged me not to leave him.

"Please don't break up our family," he pleaded.

But, I wasn't the one breaking up our family, he was the one single-handedly tearing us apart. Seeing him with her broke my heart. Gabe was the only man I ever knew, the only one I'd ever been with, and I didn't want anyone else. It's funny how you tell yourself what you won't put up with until you are faced with the situation. If Gail thought I was walking away and handing her my man without a fight, she had another thing coming. It wasn't going to happen on my watch. Not after I'd put in years of blood, sweat, and tears and molded him into the man she now wanted. I wasn't eager about letting him go to some woman who hadn't put in the work to build the family, just because she decided to open her legs for him. No. We had three kids, and too many years, between us for me to just walk away and she couldn't have him. I refused to go down without a fight. But, my mind and my heart were speaking two different languages and I ended up letting the hurt speak for me. I lashed out. I cried. I blamed myself, wondering why I wasn't enough for him when he was everything to me? I was so hurt and confused. I studied all of the information the private investigator gave me about her, trying to figure out what made her better than me. She was pretty, but she wasn't cuter. She wasn't financially established, Gabe had started giving her money here and there. On paper, she was a mess. I sat around for months, depressed, trying to figure it all out, wanting to understand what she had on me.

When I finally worked up enough courage to ask Gabe the hard questions about the affair, he did a lot of hemming and hawing, never wanting to say that she captured him with sex, did things to him I wouldn't do, and talked to him in ways I couldn't. But, that was his fault because *he* taught me. It made me feel inadequate and small, like I will never be enough for him. After all, what do you expect from someone as sexually experienced as she? The private investigator informed me that the woman who placed the call to me was an ex friend of Gail's who, apparently, knew how much she wanted Gabe and didn't agree with it.

Gail had plans to start a family with him but didn't tell him what she was doing and he stupidly believed her when she told him she was on birth control. She was a beautiful woman, used to getting her way and had set her sights on taking Gabe from us in the worst way. But, when Gabe told her that he loved his family and couldn't leave, she decided not to mention the baby and dropped Donna off at our door, walking away without a word. I was forced to raise this child, who was a product of two grown ass, irresponsible people that were too immature to stay away from each other.

Gail's disappearance left us to try to figure out how to handle having a new baby around. I was resentful, but knew that it wasn't Donna's fault that she was selfishly brought into this world by a woman who used her as a tactic to keep a man that didn't belong to her. Gabe instantly fell in love with Donna, so I loved her. I raised her.

In hind sight, I was tougher on her than the other children, but it was because she was a constant reminder of Gail, and as she grew, her mother's features became more and more prominent. It was hard to look at her, this beautiful mixture of Gabe and Gail, and when I would see Gabe catering to her, it would make me mad because all I saw was him catering to Gail. I know it was petty, but, I wouldn't give her a key to the house because I didn't want Gail to have a key to the house. I would leave her in the mall looking for me, because I wanted Gail to cry those same tears she cried. I wanted Gail to feel the pain she once caused me and I took it out on Donna.

When I found out that Sam took her to the store after I told her I wasn't going to take her, and he was killed, it was like Gail took something from me once again and that made me resent Donna even more. But, it wasn't her fault.

I'm proud of the woman she has become, and the strength in her character. She has turned out to be nothing like her birth mother, and adopted everything that is good about Gabe. Maybe my death will finally give her the answers she needs. I made sure that I gave the attorney a handwritten letter for her that explains my actions. I never fully apologized, though I should have, and I hope, at the very least, my death, and my letter, will give her some peace.

DOMESTIC VIOLENCE AWARENESS

Domestic violence *is never okay and can vary dramatically in severity and frequency. It can include physical, psychological, and/or emotional trauma. Help is out there. If you find yourself in danger, please call* **911**. *For anonymous and confidential help, contact the National Coalition Against Domestic Violence (NCADV) at:*

800.799.SAFE (7233)
800.787.3224 (TTY)

WHEN HONEYSUCKLES FALL SERIES

Eight Moments is a part of the *When Honeysuckles Fall* series. To stay up-to-date on new releases, and to be eligible for exclusive first looks, first chapters, etc. of upcoming novels, join the mailing list at:

WhenHoneysucklesFall.com

Donna's signature shirts are also available for purchase.

To purchase your *Unapologetically Me* t-shirt and accessories, visit:

ImUnapologeticallyMe.com

CARMEN HENDRIX

Born and raised in Jackson, Mississippi, Carmen Hendrix began writing at an early age. She is an avid volunteer and very active in community outreach.

Carmen's road to becoming a published author was not an easy one, and her life is reflected in her writing. Throughout her years, Carmen's love affair with words has never wavered and she further cultivated her relationship with writing through the poetry circuit in Mississippi and Texas.

Carmen hopes her writing connects with you as she tackles life's issues, including forgiveness and redemption, and she welcomes you with opened arms into her world.

Current Titles:
When Honeysuckles Fall
Eight Moments

Upcoming Title:
Phoenix Blooms

Stay up-to-date.
Visit Carmen's website for details:
CarmenHendrix.com

CPSIA information can be obtained
at www.ICGtesting.com
Printed in the USA
LVHW08s0502201018
594256LV00020B/405/P

9 780997 806021